Makeover Magic

Kelly McKain

USBORNE

L + J + T
= BFF

My
totally secret
journal

by

Lucy Jessica Hartley

JJ

ALEX
KEEP
OUT!!!

SD is the
Prince of
Pillockdom!

<u>Monday the 8th of</u>
<u>November at 6.42 o'clock,</u>
which is the exact minute
of me starting this journal.

So, I'm *Lucy Jessica Hartley*, and this is my
journal about me. I'm going to tell you all about
my life and the stuff that happens in it (and the
stuff that **DOESN'T**, most likely!). I'm even going
to tell you secret things that only Jules knows, or
sometimes even that no one except me knows.

Okay, so...

✦ My Life ✦

Worst Thing: When Mum and Dad separated in
September and Dad went to live with Uncle Ken
and Mum cried for a month. That was also the
month when we ate mainly lasagne because Mum

was too upset to cook and that's the only thing I know how to make.

Best Thing: When Delia (my nan, but she doesn't like me and Alex to call her Nan 'cos she says it makes her feel old) gave me my own sewing machine for my last birthday, when I turned 12 (only 9 months and 11 days of **NOT** being a teenager. Jules is already 13 — soooooo unfair!).

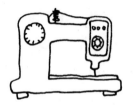

Secret Wish: To be a proper, real fashion designer. Shhh!

Secret Worry: That I am a freak of nature and I will not get my Q until I'm like 24 or something. Double shhh! *(Q means period. Me and Jules were going to say P but we have changed the letter to Q so it's more secret, and we can talk about it even when boys are there.)*

Mi Familia: You know how some people go on

about their parents being embarrassing? Well, my mum's totally not, most of the time, although she worries that she is. But my dad, who thinks he's really cool, is beyond embarrassing and out the other side. Mum says he's going through a midlife crisis. I don't entirely get what that is, but it basically means that he wants to be a rock star instead of the manager of our local Sainsbury's. Alex is my little brother…nuff said.

Bra Size: Not even telling **YOU** that, but put it this way, when I went to get my first bra a couple of weeks ago, and I was trying them on in the shop, my mum yelled out of the changing room, "Excuse me, have you got anything smaller?" (Okay, so sometimes she *is* a bit embarrassing!)

My BFF: (Best Friend Forever, not Boring Fogie Friend) is – take a deep breath – Julietta Garcia Perez Benedicionatorio. Or Jules, to most people.

Jules's mum calls her Julietta, but she says it like Who-lyetta. I like to listen for it when they are having their loud arguments in really fast Spanish, which they do quite a lot, even when you're standing right there in between them drinking a lemon Fanta.

Jules's mum is called Isabella and her dad is called Gabriel, like the angel. I can't imagine *my* dad being called after an angel.

Jules has also got a dog called Hombrito and a little brother and sister who are twins and are called Benito and Benita, plus (drum roll, please) a **très** lush elder brother called Juan-José (JJ for short). JJ is 14 and he is a total heart-throb. Sadly he has a v. babelicious girlfriend called Suzanna who…well, put it this way, her mum would never have to yell, "Excuse me, have you got anything smaller?" about bras out of changing rooms. And also she most likely got her Q at 10 or 9 or something.

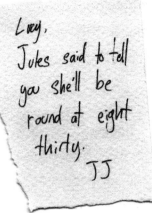

Lucy,
Jules said to tell you she'll be round at eight thirty.
JJ

BUT JJ did write me a note yesterday, which I kept.

For a bit I thought it might be a secret love message, because my horoscope said to "look beyond the obvious".

But then, today at school when I kept trying to wink at JJ in the corridor he just asked me if I had something in my eye, so maybe it's not (boo!).

I also have:

Bit of chewy JJ gave me on the bus

I wanted to keep it so I slid it up my sleeve and had to pretend to be chewing all the way home.

I also fished JJ's old bus pass out of the Garcia

Perez Benedicionatorios' kitchen bin. But I wouldn't have bothered if it'd been under something gross like spaghetti-Os, so I know I'm not obsessed or anything.

Yeah, so a bonus of being Jules's BFF is that sometimes I get to see JJ coming out of the shower wearing only a really weeny little towel (or maybe it's a large flannel).

I try to act like I don't notice JJ, 'cos of Suzanna with the big you-know-whats, but it's a bit hard when every time I see him I go burning red and have to cough and pretend I'm choking on a bit of sandwich. I don't think Jules believes me, especially in the middle of the corridor when I have no sandwiches on me. Maybe I should make extra sandwiches and have them ready to quickly eat and pretend to choke on when I see JJ coming. But then he might think I'm always scoffing my face, or what if seeing him makes me go so wibbly I shove in the sandwich but then start choking for real and then what if I just, like, **DROP DEAD** right there in the corridor? That would be *totally* embarrassing.

My one really big problem is that JJ usually sees me in my school uniform. And, I mean, I've done the best I can, but it's this really dodgy bottle-green gear that makes you look like a boy scout. I said so to Mrs. Phillips our form teacher and she said, "Well, if you don't like the green, you can always choose the rust-coloured pullover instead." So I was like, "Ooooh, thanks a lot." I mean, the colour is actually called RUST. That's like wearing a colour actually called MOULD or VOMIT or something. I know they want to make us wear this yukorama kit so we don't get distracted from our work in lessons by fancying each other – but really, who are they kidding? All the boys in my class are totally from the Kingdom of Nerdonia. Okay, maybe not Jamie Cousins, or Bill Cripps, and actually even Ben Jones is okay but mostly they are just immature idiots.

As the fashion guru of the school, here are...

My 5 Top Tips For Making Your Gross Uniform Bearable

1. Roll up the waistband of your skirt (yeah, I know everyone knows that one, but still...).
2. Wear a colourful scarf and "forget" to take it off in lessons.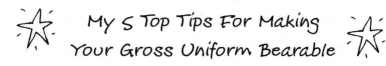
3. Wear loads of colourful friendship bracelets, but roll down your sleeves when you see Mr. Cain on the warpath. *(Every school has a Mr. Cain, even if he is not specifically called Mr.*

Cain. The Mr. Cain is the one teacher who, instead of spending breaktime drinking coffee and photocopying things, thinks it is their job to be the school Uniform Police. The Mr. Cain stands in the walkway between the main school and the mobile food-science block and points at you as you squeeze by, going, "Shirt" (meaning tuck it in), "Tie" (meaning pull it out), "Make-up" (meaning take it off), "Blazer" (meaning put it on) and even, "'School Sucks' badges are not part of the school uniform and I think you know that, Danny Jacobs. See me for detention after school" (meaning "School Sucks" badges are not part of the school uniform and I think you know that, Danny Jacobs. My store cupboard needs cleaning out and I can't be bothered to do it myself). If he could, Mr. Cain would have us all wearing long socks and straw

13

boaters and probably saying "golly-gosh"
and "boaty-o" while wearing
absolutely no make-up whatsoever.)

4. Wear purple nail polish on Mondays and claim
   you forgot to take it off after the weekend
   (don't forget to chip it a bit for extra
   believable-ness).

5. Set new trends with your tie and see how long
   it takes everyone else to catch on. But don't try
   setting the trend of having a kipper, because no
   one will catch on. Only Year 7s on their
   first day have those, and people whose mums
   still dress them in the morning (i.e. Simon
   Driscott).

6. Wear really bright pattery socks.
   If Mr. Cain complains, you can
   always offer to take them off –
   but make sure you mention
   your raging verrucas and
   athlete's foot first.
   Wow! That was 6 tips in actual fact.

Actually my mum's a bit funny about make-up as well. She says I should enjoy the fresh, natural look now while I am a *jeune fille* and that there'll be plenty of time for loading on the slap like Barbara Cartland (er, who?) when I get older. Sometimes she gets annoyed at me when I get home, because maybe a bit of blue eyeliner or glitter nail polish has accidentally got on me at lunchtime in the loos, when some of the Year 8 girls are doing swaps and that (well, you've got to try the stuff out first before you trade, haven't you?).

Mum lets me dress up for discos and parties, though, luckily, because I can't be a proper fashion designer when I grow up and not be into make-up, can I? That's half the thing, especially when it comes to the runway shows (runway is American for catwalk, **BTW**) (**BTW** is English for By The Way, **BTW**). So, experimenting with different looks is important educationally for me. Mrs. Stepton says it is "Vacuous Activity" when she's shooing us

15

out of the loos into the playground for some "Fresh Air And Exercise" and, strangely enough, when I try to explain that actually for me, experimenting with make-up is like career development, she doesn't really get what I'm on about.

Anyway, I've got to go and see Dad now. I'm not all that bothered about going, to be honest, but I have to take Alex, plus I've seen this gorge purple cotton in the fabric shop (I'm working on a design for a skirt to wear to the school disco on Saturday night) and it's pretty pricey.

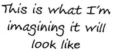

This is what I'm imagining it will look like

I've got this top to go with it

16

Dad's been good for a bit of cash since he **CRUELLY ABANDONED** us (Mum calls it guilt money) so if I can get 20 quid out of him I'll probably have enough with my savings too.

Byeeeeeeee!

Tuesday

after tea when Alex (amazingly!) had an actual good idea which will make me into a
Stand-up Babe.

Well, Dad gave me some cash, but only £8.50, even though I made myself look really **CRUELLY ABANDONED** when I asked. So I bought the material and I've been lying here on my bed looking at mags to get new inspiration for my design, because I couldn't afford enough fabric to do the skirt I showed you before.

Actually I've got sidetracked and started doing this quiz in this one mag my cousin sent me from Florida called "Are you a Stand-up Babe?" I think that's probably American for being a kind and brave person, like the sort of person who would be in Gryffindor if Harry Potter was true life, and it says:

I automatically went to tick A, but now I'm thinking of Matilda-Jane and what happened in the loos at school today.

Basically Matilda-Jane is this new girl in our class. Her dad has moved over here from Holland and he is actually Hollandish (hang on, I think I mean Dutch). Her mum was in fact English but she died when Matilda-Jane was little. I only know that because Mrs. Phillips made Matilda-Jane stand up in front of the class and introduce herself, not because we've really chatted or anything. To be honest, not that you should say stuff like this, but she's a bit…well, she looks like this:

Plaits

Kipper tie (serious blooper at Tambridge High)

Home-knitted baggy jumper in the boy scout green, yum!

Long skirt

Well, what happened was that it was the end of lunchtime and I'd been outside doing French skipping to find out which boy Jules fancies by which letter of the alphabet I tripped up on, which was X, weirdly, so...????? (What possible name begins with X?) Anyway, the bell went and Jules ran off to tell Charlie P something about drama club so I was going in on my own when I saw Mrs. Stepton coming up the corridor. I suddenly realized I still had a bit of eyeliner and lipgloss on by accident (you see, I'd been having such a good time outside getting my "Fresh Air And Exercise" that I forgot to take it off before the bell) so I ducked into the loos and there was Gina Fulcher and her lot kicking Matilda-Jane's bag around the floor. She kept trying to get it and they kept passing it around.

It's really annoying when people do that because for all they know there could be something **FRAGILE** or **BREAKABLE** inside like, say, a jar of your great grandmother's ashes, and they would just stupidly wreck it, just to be idiots. Matilda-Jane went really red and then she started crying but Gina Fulcher just laughed and said,

"Cheer up, it's only a joke. Can't you take a joke?"
But they didn't do it so hard after that. Because I
was at the sinks wiping the make-up off I saw
when Matilda-Jane grabbed the bag and dashed out
the door in front of me. She didn't talk all through
music, although she seemed sort of okay, but then
when her dad came to get her (he comes right up
to the gate like it's junior school or something) she
just burst out crying again.

So, I was saying about the quiz, I really want
to be:

A) Try to help her out.

So, I'm thinking maybe it would make a
difference if Gina Fulcher had been having a go at
Matilda-Jane in a restroom (restroom is American
for loos, BTW). I told myself I would probably be
braver in a restroom or just in America generally
or if Gina Fulcher was American, so I nearly ticked
A again.

But I kind of know it's not really about what
room it happens in, or if the bully is American or

whatever. The fact is Gina Fulcher doesn't get on my case at all and I don't want her to start. So in fact I am a C. Maybe I am even a B.

Eeeeeekkkkkk!

I've just checked and Bs get zero points, whereas to be a Stand-up Babe you have to get 35 to 40 points. Maybe I'm not the sort of person I think I am. The problem is that the stupid quiz doesn't tell you how to help. I can't help by punching Gina Fulcher. Gina Fulcher is way bigger than me for a start. I can't tell a teacher 'cos maybe Gina Fulcher will find out and punch me. Anyway, I am a sensitive and creative person who knows that violence is not the answer to the world's problems, so any punching would not help, not really. But what can I do? I can't just start going round with Matilda-Jane myself, 'cos Jules is my best friend and she'd have a hissy fit if she thought I was going off – and anyway, Matilda-Jane seems kind of geeky, so it might not be that much fun.

I told Mum about it at tea and she thought for a bit and then she said, "Well, how about trying to help her fit in more?"

Then Alex said, "You could change her like that girl off *Grease* where she's all trendy at the end, and she smokes and that." And I was about to say, "Thanks for your superb *(not)* suggestion but 8 year olds can't possibly know anything about proper problems," when I thought, hang on, for this one time he is RIGHT. So instead of being mean I just said, "It's called a makeover, you pants-brain."

Mum went to get the ice cream out of the freezer and on the way she said, "What a great idea, Alex, good thinking – except about the smoking, of course."

And I was like, "Cool it, Mum, it's not like he's just solved world hunger or anything."

So I have ticked A because I am going to be a Stand-up Babe starting from now. I am going to give Matilda-Jane a makeover so people will like her and she can get some friends. And I am going to do it tomorrow after school when Jules is at drama club so she won't find out.

Wednesday night

I really, really want to tell you how the Makeover Plan went but I am meant to be doing my homework...
Oh I know, hang on...

I got this report sheet for the science experiment we are supposed to write up for Mrs. Stepton's homework, but I'm going to write a report about something more interesting instead. I have to hand it in, but when I get it back I will stick it in here.

Year 8 Science. Set 2.

Name: Lucy Jessica Hartley

              aka The Style Goddess

Title: Operation Makeover

              Matilda-Jane   *What a stoopid*
                                              question, considering
Objective: ← Makeover Matilda-Jane   *the title!*

Equipment: One nice but untrendy girl.

              Fash mags. Money for bus into town.

Describe what you did:

  Well, the Makeover Plan was great at first, but

it all went REALLY wrong in the end (oh, hang

on, I should put that in the "Evaluate your

work" section later, sorry!). I'll start at the

beginning, or you won't know what I'm on about.

Matilda-Jane came round after school. When

I asked her over she looked at me funny,

'cos we haven't exactly spoken very much, so I

said it was because she is super brainy and I wanted to do homework together. She took my number and her actual <u>dad</u> rang up to check it was okay. Of course my mum said of course because she is cool like that.

So, we were in the kitchen and my mum went, "Would you like a Coke, girls?"

And Matilda-Jane went, "Oh, not for me, I'm not allowed fizzy drinks. I'll just have a glass of water, if that's all right, thank you, Mrs. Hartley."

And my mum went, "Certainly, no problem, Matilda-Jane, dear. Call me Sue." My mum was beaming at her like she was her long-lost actual daughter and I was some scruffy replacement she'd got muddled up with in the hospital. So I took Matilda-Jane up to my room before Mum could whip out the adoption papers or something.

Matilda-Jane started getting out her homework books while going, "Your mum is so lovely." And she said thanks for inviting her over and then she said how she was beginning to think all the girls at Tambridge High were as nasty as Gina Fulcher before then, and then she asked if we should start on the maths first or the science?

And that was when I revealed that we were actually not doing any homework. (This also explains why I haven't done the _specific_ science that's supposed to be on this report, but hopefully when you read this, Mrs. Stepton, you will totally get why this is more important, and not Vacuous Activity, as you like to say.) So anyway, I explained about the Makeover Plan. Matilda-Jane just looked really confused, like she didn't know what I was on about. So I said, "You know, make-up and hair and clothes and that?" and I got out some of my magazines to show her what I meant.

"But why would you want to change me?" asked Matilda-Jane.

I went red then, and said about seeing Gina Fulcher kicking her bag round the loos and how I felt bad for not being a Stand-up Babe. And I said how I wanted to be one, so I thought if I could make her fit in more then...

"Oh. Okay," said Matilda-Jane, in a wibbly-wobbly voice. We looked through the mags then and I thought she'd be really happy, but she just stuck her chin out and her eyes went all watery and she said, "But I like being me the way I am. I want people to like me for myself not because of how I look."

I was really hurt about that, 'cos I was only trying to help, but I didn't show it. Instead I just said, really grown-up-ly, "Well, excuse me for bothering to care but if you just change a bit on the outside then people will want to get to know you, then they'll see what a nice person you are on the inside and how you're not a boring baby just because your dad comes right up to the school gate to pick you up."

Then she was a bit silent for a while, which I think was because she was busy looking at the makeovers, like:

Rosie Simmons **loves** her new look!

After

Before

"Boys never used to ask me to parties," she says, tossing her sleek new hairstyle, "but now they do – all the time."

"That just proves how shallow most boys are," grumbled Matilda-Jane. "Besides, I don't care about them anyway. My daddy says there's plenty of time for all that when I'm 18."

I was about to give up on the whole idea and just get her to help me with my maths, which quite honestly I am not that good at, when she spotted this picture:

Now we've shown Fleur how to mix funky vintage finds from charity shops with trendy bargains from the High Street, she's got the confidence she always wanted!

Matilda-Jane blinked at the picture. "I've always wanted confidence, too," she said shyly. And that's when I knew the Makeover Plan was going to work.

So we went into town and had a look round the shops. The charity shops they visited to get stuff for Fleur in the magazine must have been in London or somewhere where rich girls give their stuff away after wearing it about 2 times. The ones in Sherborne were full of old ladies' nylon dresses that smelled like mothballs. There were some nice velvet jackets, but they released this weird smell when you put them on. Still, we found some groovy second-hand Levis hiding under a pile of geography-teacher trousers, a couple of cool shirts and a tight grey cardi that would look really good on its own with no T-shirt under, but Matilda-Jane said no way was she wearing anything without a T-shirt and vest under (a <u>vest</u>, I mean, <u>hello</u>?) so I got that for myself.

Obviously at school we have to wear our gross-omatic uniforms so Matilda-Jane is still going to look not that nice. But then I had an idea. I told her she could make her debut at the school disco, looking fabulous, and she could walk in wearing high heels like the girl off Grease, like Alex said, but without the smoking and sort of go, "Hey, Fellas," while all the boys' mouths drop open.

Matilda-Jane said that was a really good idea, apart from saying the Fellas thing. I said, "Well, it might not work without saying the words, but whatever, it's your makeover – at least we will have the high heels."

"High heels?" she croaked. "Lucy, I don't think—"

"It'll be great!" I said quickly. "Look." Then I whipped out my notebook and did her this picture really quickly like swish, swish, swish, how you see fashion designers do $\longrightarrow$

"Oh," said Matilda-Jane. "Well... If you think so."

"Trust me, I'm a fashion guru," I said and marched her into New Look before she could go all shaky-watery again.

36

We had such a laugh trying on stuff in the changing rooms. We got the sillies, as Mum calls it, and we couldn't stop giggling and dancing about in the communal bit. So – NEWSFLASH! – Matilda-Jane is quite fun after all. She tried on this brilliant black dress with sequins on the front that would be great for the disco and we wanted some sparkly jewellery to go with it but there was nothing quite right, so I said, "I know, I'll make you some."

Matilda-Jane had some saved-up pocket money on her so she got the dress and a couple of cool tops with hippy flowers on them from the sale rack. I just got a pack of hairbands 'cos I know what I'm wearing already (well, sort of, still don't know how

I'm doing the skirt), and then we went into Boots to try on make-up and test out the different body sprays.

We didn't get back to mine till 5.30. I gave Matilda-Jane a swirly-pattern scarf to tie round the second-hand jeans to make them more hippy-chick and a long floaty skirt Nan (oops, I mean Delia) bought me that isn't really my style. The skirt was sooooo Matilda-Jane's (new) style 'cos she changed into it straight away, and put on one of the flowery tops and tied the swirly scarf from the jeans round her head. So, Mrs. Stepton, now I will put it in that sciency way you like: We can <u>observe</u> that the <u>result</u> was that Matilda-Jane totally got into the makeover idea by the end, and <u>therefore</u> my <u>predictions</u> were

<u>accurate</u>. So anyway, she was just getting her books together when I had another good idea. (Please also note, Mrs. Stepton, that's 3 good ideas in one single science report. You might like to think about maybe giving me a house point? Just suggesting.) "I think you should have a name makeover as well," I said, "because, no offence, but Matilda-Jane does make you sound like the sort of girl who goes to bed at 9 o'clock and does all her homework on time."

"Okay, if you think so," she said, "but make it a short name, because I have to go soon. Daddy likes me to be home by 6 so that I can have supper and get my homework done before 9."

"What's at 9, Vice Squad?" I said.

"Bedtime."

"Oh."

I give up. I promised to help but I didn't promise not to put my foot in it, did I? (Luckily!)

We thought of MJ and Tilly and Matty and just Jane, or even Jay, and then I thought of Tilda, after the actress who was in that art exhibition sleeping in a glass case. (How cool would that job be, apart from if you start dribbling or snoring or something?!) So we went for that. We were just coming down the stairs when the doorbell rang and it was JULES.

She looked at me and she looked at Tilda in my clothes with the shopping bags, and she looked at me again, not-nicely. I started talking really quickly about the makeover idea and the school disco and the Grease Plan (but without the smoking), but she still got in a huff. "You wouldn't LEND that skirt to me and now you're GIVING it to her!" she yelled. "You're supposed to be MY best friend, in case you hadn't noticed!" Then she said something in really fast Spanish that sounded like, "Kay clase demehor amiga airez too? Kay tey pasa?"

I don't know what it meant, but I know it didn't mean, "Oh, Lucy, how kind of you to help Tilda get some friends. What a nice person you are."

Before I could think of anything to say even in English, Jules had flounced off, slamming the door. Mum came into the hall to see what the fuss was about and Tilda

41

looked like she might start crying, so I put
on a big smile and I said, "Oh, it's nothing.
It's just Jules being Jules. She'll get over it."

Draw a labelled diagram
(please use your ruler):

Jules mad
with me

Me worried

Tilda
scared of
Jules

Evaluate your work:

Makeover - 10 out of 10.

Best Friendliness with Jules - 0 out of 10.

When Mum went to drive Matilda-Jane, sorry

Tilda, home I texted Jules a load of smiley faces, but she didn't reply. I know she's really mad because she's turned her phone actually <u>off</u>. I know it looked like I was going off with Matilda-Jane (Tilda) but I soooooo wasn't. Falling out with Jules makes me feel really queasy inside, you know like when you eat too much fish and chips? I really hope she gets over it soon. It's only been one hour and I miss her already.

An epic effort, but next time I'd prefer you to write up the experiment we did in class. You know, the one with the Bunsen burner and the potassium permanganate? You were there, Lucy, remember?

Mrs. Stepton

43

Thursday

after school and after
going to see Dad.

Well, today at school Tilda didn't look any different
– you'd never know we'd done all that making over.
But that is the fun thing – everyone will have to just
wait for the disco, and then be **AMAZED**. I'm really
glad it's on this actual Saturday though, 'cos Gina
Fulcher is still being a horrible cow to Tilda. At
least Tilda hung round with me today and so Gina
left her alone apart from just saying stuff quite
loudly in the lunch queue. We pretended not to
hear and kept talking about *Friends* and laughing
loudly so GF would know we didn't care. I also
pretended not to notice Tilda's eyes going all red
and watery or when her voice went a bit choky.

Jules didn't talk to me *all day*, and she was
really annoyed when she saw me talking to Tilda.
But, I couldn't leave Tilda on her own, could I?

Not with Gina Fulcher being like that. I'm trying to be a Stand-up Babe and look after her a bit until the disco. So I knew Jules was madder than ever, and she spent breaktime with Augusta Rinaldi's lot, who all think she is completely the **BEE'S KNEES**.

That's quite a weird saying – I mean, do bees have actual knees? I might ask Mrs. Stepton if they do. Usually I'm rubbish at science but she was quite encouraging about my report on Operation Makeover Matilda-Jane. She put that it was an epic effort, which means as good as films like *Lord of the Rings* and that. Anyway, whether bees have knees or not, Augusta's sporty lot think Jules is a groovy babe, which she is, so by home time I was ready to do some serious grovelling.

Our last lesson was science so I really quickly wrote up the experiments on, erm, well it was something about sugar water in a test tube, and then I made Jules a certificate in the back of my book. (As I did so well on my homework report, I'm sure that Mrs. Stepton won't mind just that one bit of work being a bit scruffy.) Then I used my protractor to make Jules's favourite thing, which is a secret between us two:

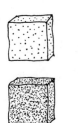

1) You take one orange and one green starburst

2) Then cut them in half

3) Then you stick an orange piece and a green piece together (bit squishy!)

So I walked part of the way home with Jules. I gave her the special Starbursts and the certificate that looked a bit like this:

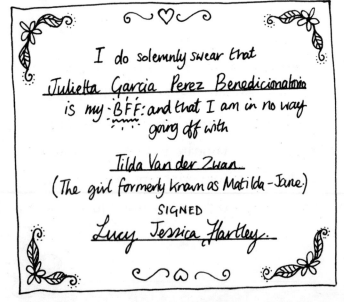

I do solemnly swear that Julietta Garcia Perez Benedicinatoria is my ·BFF· and that I am in no way going off with

Tilda Van der Zwan
(The girl formerly known as Matilda-Jane.)
SIGNED
Lucy Jessica Hartley.

This is just a copy I quickly did

Jules put the certificate in her bag and she let me have one of the special Starbursts. Then she said, "Okay, to be my friend again, you have to answer these questions:

1. Who is your Best Friend Forever, Amen?
2. Who do you want to help look cool for the school disco?
3. Who do you fancy?"

Of course I said "Jules" to the first 2 straight away. But I didn't know what to say about the third one — that's because I fancy You-Know-Who who is the actual brother of You-Also-Know-Who and I can't tell her that, can I?!

(Answer: NO WAY!)

So, I thought I would say Ben Jones or Bill Cripps or Jamie Cousins or one of the other okay boys in our class, but then I had a better idea. Instead I said, "I will say who but you will have to say who first. Who is your Mr. X?"

Jules went really bright red and her mouth sort

of opened and closed a bit without any words coming out. So in the end I didn't have to say anyone because she wouldn't tell me hers. But Jules did say she'd text me 2 letters of her Mr. X's name every day and then I can guess and he will no longer be a Mr. E. *(Mr. E = mystery, get it?! Ha ha.)* That could take ages, though, especially if Mr. X's name is anything like as long as Jules's, so I told her that maybe I'll just ask Charlie P in history (when he sits behind me), because he talks to Jules a lot about drama club so he might have some ideas about Mr. X. And Jules went, "No! Don't do that! 4 letters! I'll text you 4 whole letters every day! Proper ones, too, not just vowels!"

So I said okay. I wonder if maybe she didn't want me to ask Charlie P 'cos she has in actual fact told him who she fancies. But if she has told a boy before she's told me I will be really **MAD** 'cos I am her **BFF**. It's not only in books that boys and girls can be **BFF**, you know. Sometimes it can actually happen in real life, and if I find out Jules is going off with Charlie P and telling him secrets about who she fancies she will be getting no smiley face texts from **ME**!!

So then we thought up this cool Goth-rock outfit for the disco using some webby black stuff Jules has at home. It will look like this:

It will look really cool with her DMs

I went to see Dad on the way home, because Mum said last night, "He misses you, Lu. Can't you pop round there more often, make a bit of an effort?"

And I said, "But Mum, I do. I made a massive effort to get that money out of him for my disco design. I had to look really CRUELLY ABANDONED and even then I only got £8.50."

Mum smiled a bit sadly and hugged me for some weird reason and then she went, "I know it's hard for you, Lu."

She's right, it *is* hard for me, because Uncle Ken's flat is on the fourth floor with no lift and when it's after school I've always got all my bags and that. Plus, it smells of feet and curry inside, and Uncle Ken leaves his huge boxers to dry on the radiator in the living room – yukorama! I found out Dad has started doing that now too, 'cos when I got there, he was sitting on the sofa supervising his pants drying and strumming his guitar, which he came and got out of our loft 2 weeks ago.

Sometimes I don't feel like I know him at all. It's as if all his Dad-ness has vanished. Like, I got there and he went, "Hi, Lucy. D'ya wanna cup of tea, or a beer?" and I had to go, "Dad, I'm 12." And he was like, "Yeah, right, course, sorry," and he stuck his head in the fridge, going, "Erm, I think there's some lemonade here somewhere." I said I'd just have the tea.

So we sat there and he seemed to think he had to ask me stuff. He never did before, I mean, we just sort of got on with things. We never had little chats. He said, "So whassup?" and I said, "Oh, you know. The normal. Nothing." But then I remembered what Mum had said about him missing me and me making an effort (and I've been thinking that maybe she meant in different ways than just getting money out of him) so I told him the whole thing about Tilda and Jules and the makeover.

Then I told him something that I hadn't even realized myself, which is that I actually *like* Tilda and that I'll miss her when she gets her new friends. And I explained how I can't tell Jules that, 'cos she'd go ape on me. Even though he kept strumming his guitar annoyingly all through me talking, Dad looked quite interested. So I thought he might actually have some good advice and I said, "What do you think I should do?"

But he just gave me this startled look, the kind that Mum calls "rabbit caught in the headlights", like I was a big truck about to turn him into road kill. After ages he said, "Well…erm…just remember, it's all about the music, kid."

Helpful, n'est-ce pas?

Sometimes I have dark thoughts about my dad. I mean, properly **DARK** ones, not just about his horrible pant habits. It's like, sometimes I think that if he's stopped loving Mum, just like that, after all this time, then who's to say he won't stop…

NOOOO! Can't write that!

Can't even think that!

La! La! La! La! La!

Okay, back to normal now. Take a chill pill.

Re-laaaaaaaaaax.

So now I've written all this down in my
journal, I'm going to put on a *Friends* video and
make some jewellery for Tilda:

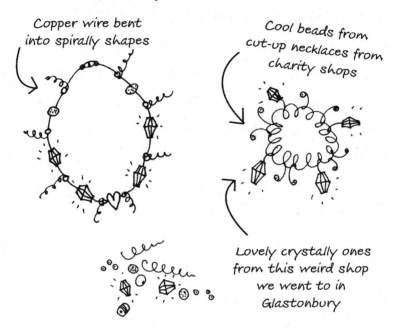

Copper wire bent
into spirally shapes

Cool beads from
cut-up necklaces from
charity shops

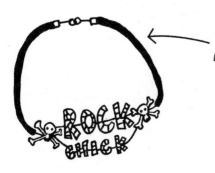

Lovely crystally ones
from this weird shop
we went to in
Glastonbury

And, of course, some for Jules like this:

I got tons of this
leather stuff from the
haberdashery (cool
word!!) stall on the
market for only
about 40p

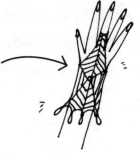

This wire is nabbed from Dad's tool box which has also been **CRUELLY ABANDONED**

I reckon Jules wants to look really cool for the disco because of Mr. X.

Yippee! My first 4 letters arrive tomorrow – then I can start solving the mystery!

Saturday

Disco Day - Yippeeeeee!!!!!!

Friday - HNSR

My first 4 letters!

Saturday - EAC

Only 3 letters?!

Jules and Tilda are coming round tonight before the disco, so hopefully I'll be able to guess who Mr. X is by then.

I phoned Jules up straight away to *complain*, because she promised 4 letters a day and she promised no vowels either, but she said, "Lu, there weren't that many more letters to choose out of, plus the *continent* I sent you is really good."

So I said, "What, do you mean it's a land mass or do you mean a consonant, as in not a vowel? And if you're saying it's really good, does that mean the name actually *starts* with a C?"

Jules just went "Erggggh" and before I could properly think, she said she had to go and collect Benito and Benita from Junior Karate and then she quickly put the phone down. So the name starts with C, hee hee. Now I've got that, Jules won't stay out of my Mr.-X-guessing clutches for long. I'll grill her when she comes round later. Got to go now – I need to work on my outfit. I've already pinned it up and I'm going to machine it now. This is what I did in the end:

I'm doing the little flowers out of material from an old top I outgrew. It'll take ages to sew them all on but it will be worth it for a secret reason, which I will write in a code:

.gnineve eht fo dne eht ta su gnitcelloc si JJ

So I'm quite glad about getting only £8.50 from Dad after all 'cos it made me have to do a short skirt. The reason this is good is because Suzanna's school skirt is microscopic so JJ must like them. But my disco one won't be as short as that. Mum wouldn't let me. When she sees girls with really short skirts, like in the park or whatever, she goes, "Was it really worth her even putting that on?" Anyway, I'll write in this journal again tonight, after the disco.

Time: Tonight

after the disco
(see, I promised, didn't I?).

Wow, so much has happened. It feels like a year has gone by in one night or something.

Well, first of all, Tilda came round and then Jules arrived already in her cool disco stuff. I gave her the necklace which she thought was fab, and she put it on straight away. But then she asked me not to tell Tilda about the Mr. X texts because it was our secret **BFF** thing. I felt bad for Tilda but I said okay because I wanted Jules to be nice to her when she came out of the bathroom with her groovy disco outfit on. I'd already done her hair and make-up like this:

sparkly slide

Superlonglash max mascara

Clip-on earrings

Moondust lipgloss

Me and Jules waited ages for Tilda. Then we waited further ages and Jules had a cheese sandwich and I had just a chunk of cheese off the block, but she still didn't come out. So finally I went and knocked on the door and after a while she unlocked it but she didn't come out. I opened the door and we went in and found her sitting on the closed seat of the loo, crying. Tilda's outfit looked great but her cheeks were streaked with black tears of Superlonglash max mascara and her nose was running into her Moondust lipgloss. My first thought was that I should have used waterproof mascara, knowing what Tilda's like about crying, and my second thought was that my first thought should not have been about mascara but about what was wrong. (Oh dear, maybe I'm still a B on the Stand-up Babe scale...) I tried to make up for it by putting my arm round her.

Jules came up and stood behind me. "Oh, no! What's up, Tilda?" she said all sweety-pie. "Is it that you don't like the outfit? After all Lucy's hard work, too. Shame!"

Now, Jules is a good actress, because of going to drama club every week and generally because of being all Spanish-ly passionate and fiery, but I am her **BFF** and she did not fool *me*. I nudged her hard in the ribs and said, "Be nice or I will mention something about someone beginning with C."

It was a bluff 'cos I hadn't worked out who it was by then, but it was obviously a good bluff 'cos it made Jules shut up.

"Daddy said I'm not allowed to go to the disco," Tilda snivelled.

"WHAT!!!" I yelled. "That's **outraaaaageous!** You should complain to the European Court of Human Child Rights!"

"So why did you come over and get all dressed up?" asked Jules.

"I just wanted to be part of things," said Tilda, all sniffly snuffly. "I thought it would be fun, the getting-ready bit, but it's made me feel worse. I was only supposed to come round to tell you I couldn't go."

They both looked at me then. But I was dead silent because I was having an **ABSOLUTE BRAINWAVE**, even better than the whole Makeover Plan (and *that* was an A1-level plan, even though it was invented by Alex).

"Tilderella, you *shall* go to the disco!" I cried and waved my arms about like a fairy godmother with a wand.

"But Daddy says…" Tilda began.

"But Daddy won't know," I said, and did my evil-genius laugh (like **HA-HA-HAAAAAA!**) while still twirling with my pretend wand. Then I knocked a bottle of shampoo off the side of the bath and a bit spilled on the floor, so I had to wipe that up first, but then afterwards I told them about...

My Strict-Parent-
Busting Plan (Sssshhhh!!)

1. Tilda rings up her dad.
2. Tilda says that I am not going to the disco either because my mum also thinks there's plenty of time for boys and parties and having any fun whatsoever when I'm 18 and until then I just have to do homework, basically. So then Tilda tells her dad we are doing the homework at my house and asks if she can stay over afterwards, because she will be just too exhausted to walk home and in fact she might accidentally fall down a manhole and break her writing arm in, like, 5 places and *then* she won't be able to study and *then* she might get keen on boys and clothes and discos and that.
3. Tilda's dad totally believes it and agrees. We all go to the disco! **HA-HA-HAAAAAA!**

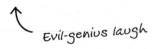
Evil-genius laugh

62

I explained this plan to Tilda and Jules and while I was telling it Jules ate another cheese sandwich. Tilda started looking happy again. "Do you think it'll work?" she asked.

"Of course," I said. "It's really subtle, like proper secret-agent ideas. Your dad will never suspect anything, not in a million, billion, gazillion—"

"We get the picture," said Jules, looking at her watch. "Just make the call, Tilda."

So Tilda rang home and her dad wanted to talk to my mum. *Eeeeekkkkk!* I did some quick thinking and told him she was in the bath but that she said it was okay. He didn't seem too happy (it was a breath-holdy moment) so I offered to get her out of the bath but he said it was all right because he spoke to her before when Matilda-Jane came over last time and he already had our address and phone number and that. "As long as your parents will be there," he said. Par*ENT*, I said, and I explained about my dad not living here and how he CRUELLY ABANDONED us because he wants to be a rock star and so he was at that moment living at Uncle Ken's practising on his guitar and watching his pants dry on the radiator and hopefully thinking of buying a Glade plug-in to get rid of the curry and feet smell and—

But Tilda's dad cut in and said, "As long as someone's at home with you girls, that's fine," so that was lucky because it saved me having to go into any real detail or anything.

Then he spoke to Tilda and she just said things like "I will" and "I know" and "I promise" in this little-girl voice. When she put down the phone we all did the evil-genius laugh together and Jules smiled at Tilda and I thought *yippeeee the Makeover Plan is working already if Jules is starting to like her.*

So I fixed up Tilda's make-up again and then she put on the high-heeled silver strappy sandals I was lending her, but she just went all wobbly, and could only walk with me and Jules holding her up on each side. Tilda said, "I don't think I can wear these," and I said, "But you have to wear them. They are vital for the Makeover Plan. If you're not doing the smoking or saying the actual words then all we have left is the wearing the high heels."

"Lu, she'll be okay in her slip-ons," said Jules. Now she was definitely being nice to Tilda. Also, it was nearly 7 and I bet she wanted to hurry up and get to the disco for some **très** mysterious reason beginning with C.

So, we all stepped out the door like models off a runway (I said that was American for catwalk already, didn't I?).

I have done these pictures of us like photos:

☆ TiLDA ☆

☆ JULES ☆

So I can now announce that the Makeover Plan
worked brilliantly even without saying the actual
words or the smoking or the high heels. When we
walked in, it took people a minute to recognize
Tilda at all and then it was like that slow-motion
thing in films but happening in real life, where

loads of people turned and looked and all the boys' mouths dropped open (well, except Simon Driscott's because he is Immune to Style).

We went over to the drinks table to get cans of Coke and Tilda got one too, even though she's not allowed fizzy drinks. The Coke must have made her go a bit hyper though, because after a few minutes Ben Jones asked her to dance and instead of being shy like usual she just grabbed his arm and rushed onto the dance floor (aka the end of the gym with the ropes against the wall). I was so busy staring at her that I didn't notice Gina Fulcher coming up to me. And this is honestly the exact thing that she said:

Gina:	Where did you get that necklace?
Me:	I made it.
Gina:	It's not bad. Could you make me one, do you think?
Me:	Only for mates.

Gina:	Aww, go on, I'll be your best friend.
Me:	Jules is my best friend, but I'll make you one if you promise to leave Tilda alone from now on.
Gina:	You mean Matilda-Jane? Okay, deal. I suppose she's quite cool, anyway.
Me:	*(Smiling knowingly as the Makeover Plan succeeds!)*

So, some people say fashion is a Vacuous Activity (you know who I mean – i.e. Mrs. Stepton), but I've *soooooo* proved that fashion creates peace and harmony and maybe even saves lives. I say *saves lives* because what if it was dark and Gina Fulcher decked Tilda outside and then Tilda went flying backwards and fell down a manhole and died? And you can't say that would never happen because every year about 2 old ladies die from leaning over their wheelie bins and then falling in and rolling down the street into traffic or whatever. That is the honest truth.

And also, you are more likely to have an accident involving your fridge than to win the lottery, so it just shows, *you never know where danger is lurking.*

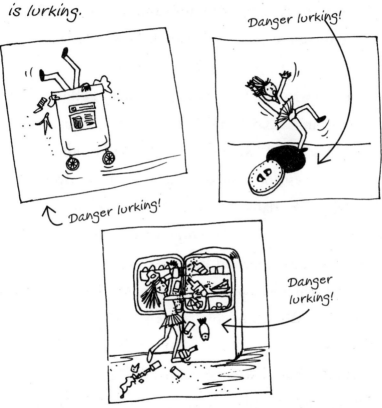

Danger lurking!

Danger lurking!

Danger lurking!

Anyway, then Jamie Cousins asked me to dance and so I said yes, because he is an okay boy and although he is not You-Know-Who, he is not from the Dukedom of Dorkovia either.

I just want to stop here for a minute and say something about boys dancing. Y-O-Y-O-Y do boys ask you to dance and then you stand there while they freak out in the middle of the floor doing some sort of demented break-dancing hoojamiwhatsit? So while I was standing there staring in ASTONISHMENT at Jamie Cousins writhing about like he was the Great Houdini trying to escape from a straitjacket, Bill Cripps asked me to dance and actually did it properly. Then some of the other boys asked me, and they were asking Tilda and Jules as well, and swapping round which was fun 'cos me and the girls could chat while we were going slowly round and round on the spot.

So I did get some good dances, and some kisses too but only on-the-cheek ones. Jules's pal Charlie P danced with Tilda and he wouldn't swap round for 3 whole songs, even though other girls were queuing up for him. I saw Jules staring at Tilda and Charlie P going round and round in the slow circle thing. Then – *newsflash!!!* – they started actually *snogging!!!!!!!!!!!!!!!!!!!!!!!*

When she saw them, Jules's eyes started actually *popping* and she went all starey and sort of gapey, like a fish. I thought maybe she was worried that Charlie P would tell Tilda who she fancied and then Tilda would tell me. I knew it wasn't because Jules fancied Charlie P or anything, because she'd texted me an S and there is no S in Charlie Perchance, is there? When I looked over at Jules she gave me this horrible stare, like she wanted to deck *me* till I fell down a manhole and died. I didn't know why then, but I found out pretty soon after. Before I tell you about that you have to know something else, though. It's the worst thing. The most embarrassing bit.

It started when Simon Driscott, the Prince of Pillockdom, came up and asked me to dance. I was about to say something out of a film like, "You and me? Dream on, babe!" but then I thought of Tilda and how there could be a really nice person lurking beneath his stonewash jeans and strange lopsided haircut, and so I said okay. But then when the song finished Simon Driscott clamped his hands on my bum and tried to snog me with tongues, so I ended up having to be a bit rude after all.

Unfortunately, there was quite a long pause before the next song came on (which proves that the school should have hired a proper DJ and not just expected Mr. Bridges to manage with a CD player and a backwards baseball cap). Anyway, the pause was just long enough for **EVERYONE** to hear me go, "Yurgh! The only way you would be snogging me with tongues would be if your name was Juan-José Garcia Perez Benedicionatorio and I don't think it is actually, is it, *Simon Driscott*?"

So everyone just went "*ooooooooohhhhhh*" and started laughing and I went red and Jules gave me this smugster look like, *I knew it, I just knew it.*

72

Anyway I'm too tired to write more now. The next bit's too sad and mad-making. I'll write again tomorrow, as soon as I wake up. Mum says things always seem better in the morning. I really, really hope she's right.

Zzzzzz z...

Time: Tomorrow,

as soon as I wake up
(while having a bit of toast
and jam and that).

Okay, so now it is time for the rest of the story,
including the bad bits. And no, it doesn't seem any
better in the morning (i.e. now).

You know I said fashion causes peace
and harmony? Well, it also
causes trouble. Even worse
than bully trouble –
BFF trouble.

So, right after the Tilda-
snogging-Charlie-P
incident (and the Simon-
Driscott-trying-to-snog-
me incident – yurgh!),
Jules ran into the loos and
I ran after her.

"What's wrong?" I asked, getting my thoughts in the right order even though I desperately wanted to mention that her mascara was running because she was crying a bit (maybe there's hope for me yet in the Stand-up Babe stakes).

"Charlie's kissing Tilda!" Jules wailed loudly.

I stared at her, totally and utterly confused. "But why do you care? There's no S in Charlie Perchance."

"But there *is* in Charles Perchance," sniffled Jules. "That's his proper name."

"You cheated!" I yelled.

"Proper name counts!" Jules wailed even more loudly. "Anyway, that's not the point, the point is—"

"You fancy Charlie P?" I shouted.

"Shhhhh!" went Jules. "Yes, I do, all right? And I thought, after all the time we've spent at drama together, well I thought maybe he was starting to fancy me back. But now he's snogging Tilda Van der Crybaby, thanks to you!"

I couldn't believe it. I went, "How is that *my* fault? It's not like I'm out there making her stuck to his face, am I?"

"Shut up!" Jules yelled. "Anyway, if you hadn't made her look all cool and trendy he probably wouldn't even have noticed her! Now he's going out with her! She's stolen my **BFF** and now she's stealing my future husband too!"

"But she's not stealing me," I went, all gobsmackedly. "And who says they're going out with each other?"

"Lucy, they snogged for ages right in front of everyone. *Hello?* Course it means they are!"

"Okay, maybe they are, but it won't last."

"Why not? You've made her into a cool girl. I was even starting to like her myself, but I'm definitely not now. And I don't like you very much either, Lucy Jessica Hartley!"

And then Jules stormed out of the loos. She's very good at storming out of places. You'd think she learned it in drama class but actually it's a natural talent. She slams doors so hard you can almost feel the walls shake. But I am only going on about that because it still makes me sad thinking of what happened. The makeover success had turned into a makeover disaster.

I followed Jules out of the loos. Then the teachers started doing the raffle, which meant the strip lights went on, so Tilda had to detach herself from Charlie P's tonsils. Jules headed over to the drinks table and Tilda spotted us and started walking over. I tried to warn her by staring hard at her and hoping I'd suddenly developed psychic powers, thinking, *Jules is mad with you! Run away!* but she didn't get it. Jules was totally seething over her raffle tickets, but Tilda must have just thought it was because she had really wanted the incomplete French shopping flashcard set and Liana Hawley won it instead. *(BTW, school raffles are all about the teachers getting rid of their junk without having to pay to hire a skip. Mr. Cain had obviously spent the entire*

77

week giving people the detention of cleaning out his store cupboard, because it was like, oh, goodie, please let me win the left-over exercise books from last year, some dusty pencils, 3rd-place rosettes and an abacus with all the blue beads missing.)

Then the raffle was over and the lights went off again and I thought that even though I had solved the Gina Fulcher problem I might have the problem of Jules actually decking Tilda outside until she fell down a manhole and died. But then Mr. Bridges put on "Smells Like Teen Spirit" really loud and there was a big mosh which we all joined in, so no one decked anyone.

And then, at last, the most important bit of the night had arrived – the end! If my secret code worked, you should know that JJ came to walk us home (whoops – I shouldn't have said that forwards!).

I had to get up close to him somehow, as, for this one time, he was not stapled to the side of Suzanna with the big you-know-whats. So when we'd all got our coats and gone outside I said, "It's so dark, let's all link arms or we might fall down a manhole and die."

The mood Jules was in, well, she wasn't going to let me get away with **THAT**. "Oh, no, Lucy," she went, doing her pretend sweet acting thingy that does not fool me for one second. "Manholes have little flashing lights on to warn you, so there's no danger of falling down them." And she sort of nudged me over away from JJ.

"Oh, no, I think you're mistaken, Julietta." (I said that to annoy her because she hates her proper name.) "I read an article in the paper about how students have nicked all the flashing lights to put on their nicked shopping trolleys to make some sort of transport for pub crawls.

So manholes *are*
dangerous, in actual fact."

Of course, I was completely making it up as
I went along, but it was totally believable because
JJ was like, "Well, just in case…"

He was about to take my arm when Jules
shoved herself in between us and linked arms with
both of us, squeezing mine so hard I went, "Ow!"
Lucky Tilda was on the other side of JJ and got to
link arms with him, not that she appreciated it,
she was probably dreaming of Charlie P and still
feeling a bit spinny from all that going round and
round on the spot that boys call dancing.

JJ leaned over Jules and said to me, "You look
great tonight, Lucy. I love the outfit."

Well, I nearly dropped right down on the pavement and DIED, manhole or no manhole. I managed to say, "Thanks, I made it myself."

"That's brill," said JJ.

 "You're so talented."

I will remember those words FOR EVER. Sadly I will also remember these next words for ever, which was Jules saying: "Yeah, it's hard to find things in the shops that fit properly when you've got such a flat chest, isn't it, Lucy?"

Well, I don't have to tell you that I would have given anything for a hazardous wheelie bin right then, just to jump into and trundle off, never to return. I still can't believe Jules said that, however mad she was! In front of JJ as well! She knows I'm really sensitive about being a *late developer* as Mum and the assistants in Marks and Sparks bra department call it. And especially when JJ is going out with the proud owner of great big you-know-whats.

"You mean, she's got a svelte figure, like a model," said Tilda shyly.

I could have hugged her, well I would have, but Jules's grip on my arm was so tight I couldn't wriggle out of it.

When we got to my house I just said thanks to JJ for walking us back and **NADA** to Jules (which is Spanish for *nothing*, BTW) then me and Tilda went in.

So, that is pretty bad, right? But Tilda and I had a bigger shock when we walked in the door. I thought *I* was angry 'cos of Jules, but there was someone even more angry than 10 Lucys put together.

Tilda's dad! *(Gulp.)*

So, *quel désastre*, Tilda's dad had brought her maths book round, thinking she'd need it, and found her *not* here, *not* doing homework with me. Mr. Van der Zwan and Mum seemed to have worked out between them what had

happened, because Mum started on me as soon
as I walked in the kitchen, going, "Lucy, how
could you put me in such an awkward position?"
She was leaning against the counter, with a cup
of coffee in her hand. It didn't look that awkward
to me, but... Then she went, "It's just not like
you to lie, love. I'm so disappointed in you."
And then I got what she meant about the awkward
position.

"But I didn't mean——" I began.

"Well, it certainly wasn't my Matilda-Jane
who started this," said Mr. Van der Zwan. He has
obviously never learned that it is rude to
interrupt. "She must have been led along by your
daughter, even to *want* to attend such an event.
I expect there were boys there – and drink, I
shouldn't wonder."

My mum sighed. "Oh, come on, Mr. Van der
Zwan, we're talking about a school disco
supervised by the teachers, not an illegal rave in
the middle of Wiltshire! The only drink available

83

would be Coke or lemonade, I'd imagine."

"Coke or lemonade?" he gasped. "Filthy stuff."
He turned to Tilda. "And what is that on your
face?" he asked.

I couldn't help being a bit proud then.
However angry he was, he'd still been distracted
by the fabulousness of the make-up job I'd done.
"I designed the make-up and hair as part of an
overall look," I explained. "It's really good stuff,
that MAC gear. Look how the mascara has stayed
put, even through the mosh at the end of the
night, which got pretty sweaty, didn't it, Tilda?
You should have seen it with the Moondust lipgloss
too, but I'm not surprised that's all worn off.
Cosmetics technology's getting better all the time,
but you wouldn't expect even long-lasting, solid
gloss shine to still be on after 3 songs' worth
of tonsil tennis."

"Lucy, shut up!" cried Tilda.

And so I did. Tilda's cheeks were burning
bright red and Tilda's dad was gaping at me. Then

he went, "The nerve! You change my daughter's name, put muck all over her face and I don't think I even want to *know* what tonsil tennis is!"

Oh, dear. Did I really say *that* in front of Tilda's dad? I thought about trying to pretend that tonsil tennis was some sort of game you play with bats and a ping-pong ball, but I knew it wouldn't help.

Then Tilda's dad got all moody with my mum, going, "Well, aren't you going to say something about this behaviour?"

"I certainly am," said Mum, putting her coffee down and standing up tall. "Lucy, I can't believe you used my best MAC make-up for a school disco!" Then she smiled at Tilda, who looked like she was about to cry. "I'm not blaming you, love, because you didn't know she wasn't allowed it. You look wonderful, by the way."

Tilda managed a small smile but Mr. Van der Zwan looked hotter and crosser than 29 hot-cross buns. "I was thinking of something more along the

85

lines of a lecture on good conduct and
solid morals, *Mrs.* Hartley," he said. "I do
understand that the boundaries needed for good
discipline can be difficult for busy single parents
to enforce, but I really think…"

My mum looked majorly angry then, and at last
not with me, *yippeeeee*!! "I will discipline my
daughter as I see fit when we have some private
family time, thank you very much," she said
spikily. "I don't believe Lucy would have had
anything other than the best intentions in trying to
fix it for Tilda to go to the disco like everyone
else. I'm not condoning the method she used,
especially when my MAC comes into it, but Tilda
has to live in the real world, Mr. Van der Zwan.
She needs friends."

"*Matilda-Jane* is much better off without
friends like your daughter," said Tilda's dad. I
couldn't believe that! He meant she was better off
without *me*! Char-*ming*! And I was the one who
had cheered her up and hung round with her, even

though it made Jules mad at me, and I was the one who came up with the Makeover Plan, well, with Alex, and I was the one who was being a Stand-up Babe and everything!

"Tilda, tell him about Gina and…" I whispered.

But Tilda just shook her head quickly, and stared at the floor, suddenly very interested in a bit of cheese Jules had dropped earlier out of her sandwich.

"Get your things, Matilda-Jane," said Mr. Van der Zwan. "We're going home. And I don't want you to play with this girl again. She is a *corrupting influence*."

"I won't have my daughter spoken about like that," said Mum, very quietly and firmly, as Tilda miserably gathered up her books and bag from the kitchen chair. When my mum goes like that it's much more scary than her shouty kind of angry.

"Fine. We're leaving, anyway," said Mr. Van der Zwan.

"Tilda, tell him about…" I started saying, but she didn't look at me as her dad marched her out of the house. He screeched the car away from the pavement as if he couldn't get Tilda away from my *corrupting influence* fast enough. I felt horrible, like I was going to throw up, and my legs went all wobbly.

Mum put the kettle on and made me a hot chocolate. We sat down on the sofa together. I could hear my heart pounding in  my ears, because I knew now that we had the *private family time* she was going to do the *disciplining*. "Mum, I'm sorry…" I began. "I know I shouldn't have lied to him on the phone but I was only trying to help."

"Well, I can see why he was angry," Mum said sternly. "If I thought you were somewhere and found you weren't, I'd be angry too, not to mention worried sick about your safety."

I spluttered some hot chocolate back into my

mug. I hadn't thought of it like that before. "I'm sorry, really," I said, honestly meaning it. "But if Tilda had told him about Gina Fulcher he might have understood better. I mean, maybe I should have just said about what was happening."

Mum smiled at me. "You've done what you can, Lu, but you can't fight Tilda's battles for her. She's got to learn to stand up for herself."

"Yeah, I know."

We were quiet for a bit after that, sipping our drinks and staring at the ads even though the TV was on mute. Then Mum said this quite weird thing. She said, "Lucy, do you think Mr. Van der Zwan's right? I mean, maybe I *am* going too easy on you because I feel like I've got to make up for your dad leaving. I've been so upset, I... Maybe all this is making me a bad mother." Like I said, it was weird. She's always been so sure of everything. Now she's started asking *me* for advice?

Eeeeeekkkkkk!

I kicked my feet up on the sofa and leaned on

her shoulder. "You're a great mum," I said, 'cos she is. "There is one thing you could improve, though."

She frowned at me, looking pretty worried. "What?"

"Well, you could be less stingy with your MAC stuff."

Mum laughed and swatted at me, going, "You're pushing your luck, young lady!"

I shrugged. "Anyway, when I'm a famoso fashion designer I'll get stacks of MAC stuff free like pop stars do and that."

Mum laughed. "Will you now? You'll be lending it to me then!"

I wanted to laugh too, but it came out all strangled-sounding. Even though Mum wasn't mad with me any more, the churning-stomach feeling wouldn't go away. I knew it wasn't only 'cos of jumping around in the mosh with 3 cans of Coke inside me. And it wasn't just about Mr. Van der Zwan either. "I can't believe I've managed to lose Jules *and* Tilda, both at once," I said, feeling myself nearly start crying. "And all because of one stupid letter S."

Mum sat me up straight and peered at me. "You've confused me, Lu," she said.

So I told her about the Charlie P disaster then, and how I could have realized and stopped it happening if Jules hadn't texted me an S for Charles and muddled up my guessing. Mum squeezed my shoulders and went, "Don't worry, love, it'll blow over. These things always do." But I'd seen the look on Jules's face. I somehow doubted it.

And I wasn't just worried about Jules. "Stupid stricty dad," I grumbled. "How does Tilda put up with him?"

"I know it's hard, Lu," Mum said, "but try and see it his way. It's difficult to accept when someone you love suddenly changes and wants to be completely different."

She looked at me funny then and I realized she

was talking about her and Dad as well as Mr. Van der Zwan and Tilda. I went all quiet then 'cos I hadn't thought about it like that before.

"I do feel for poor Tilda, though," Mum said, after a while. "Isn't it strange? She just wants to be a bit more grown up, but then once people *are* grown up they sometimes want to be 16 all over again."

Now I definitely knew she only meant Dad, because Mr. Van der Zwan looks like the sort of person who was never 16 and just kind of went from 10 years old to 43 overnight. "Is that what Dad's playing at?" I asked.

Mum sighed and slurped her hot chocolate and then she said, "I think he wants his choices again."

"Stupid idiot," I grumbled. "Why would he even *want* the choice of sitting in a smelly flat playing the guitar and watching his pants dry? We're a way better choice than *that*. Besides, he chose us first, so he should just stick to it."

Mum shifted on the sofa. "Feelings aren't

always as simple as that, Lu," she said, all tired-outly. "In a way, I do understand it."

"Well, don't let him know that, will you?" I huffed.

Mum winked at me as I handed her my empty mug. "Don't worry," she said, "I won't!"

Apart from not letting me use her MAC stuff, I don't know how Mum could even doubt for one tiny microsecond that she is the best mum in the universe. I wish she could sort things out with Jules and Tilda for me. But I know that's something I'm going to have to do for myself.

Monday

Well, today has been a total roller-coaster ride of emotionality.

What happened was:

FIRSTLY, Jules was sad because she thought Tilda was going out with Charlie P.

SECONDLY, Jules was happy because Emily Jackson said Tilda isn't allowed to go out with Charlie P, 'cos her dad said

 NO BOYS.

THIRDLY, Jules was angry because she was about to go up to Charlie P in maths, when Emily Jackson *herself* passed him a note asking him out.

FOURTHLY, Jules was relieved because Charlie P said no to Emily Jackson and told Ben Jones to tell her it was because he liked someone else.

FIFTHLY, Jules was hopeful in case it was her and nervous in case it wasn't her.

SIXTHLY (how do you say that? Sixethly, sicethly? Six-thely? Weird or what?!), Jules was ecstatic because Ben Jones told Augusta Rinaldi it *was* her.

SEVENTHLY, Jules was about to go up to Charlie P, but then Jamie Cousins came over from him and told Jules that Charlie P was going to go out with Emily Jackson after all, because her dad had an extra ticket to the Southampton v Liverpool match on Saturday and she said she'd take *him* if he did.

EIGHTHLY, well, there wasn't an eighthly because Mr. Bridges said, "Will you lot please stop wandering around whispering and get on with your work! Just because I was a cool and groovy DJ on Saturday night doesn't mean I will have nonsense in my classroom now!"

To put his mind at rest, I nearly said, "Don't worry, Sir, no one thought you were a cool and groovy DJ," but he'd said silence till the bell, so I didn't. Also I didn't want anyone to think about the disco too hard in case they remembered the thing that had happened with me saying really loudly about You-Know-Who.

I tried to find Tilda at break (she's in the super-brainy maths set, which I am NOT, so I couldn't talk to her during all the wandering around not getting on with our work) but she was utterly nowhere. But when I was by the water fountain, I did see actual JJ himself. He came up to me and said, "Did you have a good time on Saturday night?"

I said, all sophisticatedly, "Yeah, thanks for walking us home. I hope you didn't fall in any manholes later on because of the students taking the lights for their shopping-trolley-pub-crawl transport like I read in the paper."

And he said, "No, we were fine thanks," and then Suzanna with the big you-know-whats came along. Just as she put her arm round JJ (boo! hiss!) that stupid idiot Simon Driscott, the Prince of Pillockdom, went by with his Geeky Minions.

The Prince of Pillockdom did the pheee-ooo-witttt-type whistle that builders do off scaffolding to my mum that makes her go all red and speed up walking. All the Geeky Minions started laughing. Well, it made me go all red and want to speed up walking or even actually run away, but I played it cool and went, "Weird. Don't know why he's doing that whistling thing when we were just talking about manholes like totally normal mates! Gotta go, bye!" and I rushed off.

I am *soooooo* going to rewire the computer room so that when the Prince of Pillockdom and the Geeky Minions go in there for their stupid club at lunchtime all the computers will

except one which will just flash up words on the
screen saying,

**GREETINGS
FROM
LUCY JESSICA
HARTLEY!!!**

and then it will do my evil-genius laugh, like **HA-
HA-HAAAAAA!**

So anyway, NINTHLY, I was in total
embarrassment.

'Cos JJ and Suzanna were still watching, I had
to look like I was rushing actually *to* somewhere
so I rushed actually *to* the loos and found Jules.
There she was looking all sad about Charlie P and
there I was looking all embarrassed about JJ so we

were nice to each other. We did our last bit of making up, even though I knew she was nearly okay in maths before because she lent me her rubber. Our last bit of making up is always saying this thing while shaking hands:

Make friends, make friends,
Never, never break friends,
If you do, you'll catch the flu,
And that will be the end of you!

It's really babyish, but we always used to say it when we were little so it's our special **BFF** thing like the orange and green Starbursts.

Then Jules went, "There's no problem now because Tilda can't talk to you anyway."

"And also because you're not going off with Charlie P after all," I said back.

"I was never going off with Charlie P," said Jules. "It's impossible to go off with boys!"

I just shrugged, like, *whatever*, but I have read books where girls are **BFF** with boys so I know it probably happens all the time.

So anyway, I sat with Jules at lunch and I let her swap places with me so she didn't have to watch Emily Jackson sharing her cheese dippers with Charlie P. Tilda came in and quite a few people asked her to sit at their lunch table but she wouldn't hardly even talk to anyone. She still looked all pale and trembly and I started to worry, because you have to watch out for people and maybe tell a teacher or even call ChildLine if you think there is something really bad happening to them.

Just in case, as Tilda went past with her lunchbox, I said, "Did your dad hit you with a big stick or something?"

Tilda looked ASTONISHED and said, "No! Daddy wouldn't do anything like that! It's just, he was so disappointed in me, it was awful."

Well, I knew how she felt because I felt awful too when Mum said about being disappointed in me on Saturday night. It was way worse than getting shouted at, but Jules just went, "Ohhh, *disappointment*. How scary – not!"

"It's not my fault we both like Charlie P," said Tilda, all snappishly, which was really unusual for her. "Anyway, if he goes out with someone just because of football-match tickets and cheese dippers then he is obviously an extr*eeeeeee*mely shallow person and both of us are too good for him, so there."

Jules looked really amazed that Tilda had stood up for herself. For once, the famous Garcia Perez Benedicionatorio mouth was shut and all was silencio.

"Anyway, I'm not allowed to talk to you, so I'd better go," Tilda said to me, and shuffled away to sit next to Mrs. Avery, the lunch monitor. *(That shows she was properly upset because no one would normally sit on the teacher table on purpose. Normally people would only ever sit there 'cos they're made to, say if they're being an idiot and putting*

chocolate mousse up their nose or something.) Poor Tilda. Well, poor Matilda-Jane. Tilda the cool girl making jokes and dancing round the changing rooms at New Look had completely vanished – ka-poof! I couldn't go over and cheer her up because she'd get in even more trouble if her dad found out.

Jules could tell how upset I was for Tilda, because when she offered me a yogurt I just went "no thanks" without even looking to see what flavour it was. And she was all quiet and thoughtful, right till the bell.

Then in English we were doing poems so Jules sent me this poemy note:

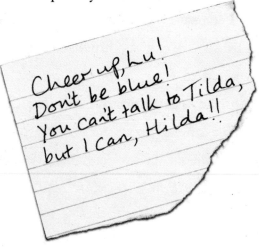

Cheer up, Lu!
Don't be blue!
You can't talk to Tilda,
but I can, Hilda!!

I don't know who Hilda is, I think it's just to make it rhyme. But, whatever, it is great that Jules has decided to like Tilda. So I wrote a poemy note back on this bus ticket I found under my chair.

Can't stick this one in 'cos Jules wrote it on her hand:

And so I leaned across and wrote, *Yeah!!!!!!!!* on her elbow.

Then we had to do working in pairs which was cool beans 'cos we could talk normally without having to rhyme. I said, "Jules, you have to get past Stricty Dad, you know, and believe me he is a tricky customer."

Jules went, "No problemo. If you did a makeover to turn Tilda trendy you can do a reverse one to turn me untrendy, *n'est-ce pas?*" I looked at the ripped tights, thick black eyeliner and long scraggly bunches of Jules and I thought, wow, my biggest challenge yet! So we did the evil-genius laugh, like **HA-HA-HAAAAAA!**, which made everyone jump and so then we got separated. Shame the Reverse Makeover Plan is super secret or we could have explained that we were not mucking about but in fact being Stand-up Babes and saving an upset lonely girl from the state of no-friendliness, but at least sitting away from Jules gave me time to get some proper work done, which was this:

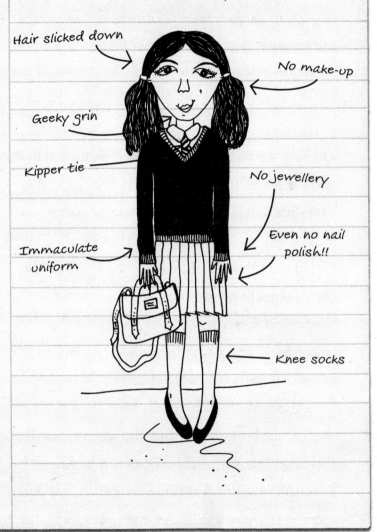

Tuesday

NEWSFLASH! Jules thought my design for the Reverse Makeover Plan was brill!

So today I brought in the knee socks from home and we made Jules into Julietta the Superswot straight away after school. It was amazing – she looked like a completely different person. We were just going "Wow!" and also I was going, "Can I copy your Unit 14b because I was so busy masterminding the Reverse Makeover Plan yesterday in class that I didn't get round to it," when Mrs. Stepton walked in.

I thought she'd be really mad about us being in the loos at home time, but she wasn't. Secretly, I reckon that's because I am sort of like her favourite now, even though teachers can't actually show it straight out. Cross my heart and hope to die (well, not die but okay maybe hope to fall down a manhole and get a really purple bruise), she was *soooooo* nice. Instead of getting huffy she just went, "You know, we really should consider putting the books and desks in here, seeing as this is where you girls spend all your time."

I said I thought that was a great idea and Jules giggled (I don't know why).

Mrs. Stepton took a deep breath and went all moody-looking. Jules is less than her favourite since we were working in threes doing refraction and reflection in the water tank with the lights off a few weeks ago. When the lights came back on most of our water was on the floor and on Jules and Charlie P 'cos they were mucking round splashing each other (**WHY** did I not notice she fancied him? I am intensely, immensely dense! – oh, look, I'm still rhyming from yesterday).

Anyway, Mrs. Stepton was about to go "shoo, shoo, out into the fresh air" and recite her Vacuous Activity speech about make-up when she properly looked at Jules and saw that there was NO make-up, **HA-HA-HAAAAAAA!**

Evil-genius laugh again!

So instead she said Jules looked *exemplary* and gave her a house point.

I said, "Ah, house points, interesting subject. Do I get one too, seeing as you didn't give me any for my brilliant science report, even though I hinted?"

Mrs. Stepton looked up and down my scruffy uniform and my accidental bits of eyeliner and lipgloss and nail polish, and sort of rolled her eyes. "Maybe next time, dear," she said.

When we went past to go out I winked at Mrs. Stepton to show I knew she couldn't look like having favourites in front of the other pupils. Then me and Jules had to run round to the main entrance 'cos Tilda's dad would be there already, and then I had to hide behind the One World display in the front lobby while Julietta the Superswot strutted her unfunky stuff.

I'm quickly writing this sitting on the loo,
BTW, while Julietta the superswot transforms
back into Jules (she said she's not walking
home like <u>that</u> and I get her point). I'm not,
like, <u>on</u> the loo but on the closed seat of the
loo. Had to tell you that in case you thought
urgh, gross, and didn't want to read this bit.
That's why my writing's a bit wobbly and also
why it's in gel pen on bog roll (I have

forgotten my journal). Mrs. Stepton was right when she said about having desks and books in here. It would be a lot easier to write this if we did. It would also be cool to get a Coke machine and actually even hot tongs to do hairstyles with. Maybe I'll mention that at the next Students Say meeting.

Our teachers are real stinge-merchants so we have this economy bog roll, which is horrible for doing what you're meant to do with it, but quite good for writing on actually. I couldn't wait till I got home in case I forgot anything and I absolutely <u>had</u> to write down now that it's all worked out BRILLIANTLY.

From my hiding place behind the One World display, I could see exactly what happened. Jules ran out of the school just as Tilda and Mr. Van der Zwan were getting in the car. She was going, "Matilda-Jane, wait! You left your research papers in the library when we were

working there at breaktime on our super-brainy project!"

Tilda's dad was just staring at her at first and then he did a huge grin. He said, "You didn't tell me you had a new friend, Matilda-Jane." And Tilda looked startled for a minute and then she said, "Yes, this is..."

And Jules went, "Julietta Garcia Perez Benedicionatorio. It's a pleasure to meet you, Mr. Van der Zwan. Matilda-Jane has told me so much about you."

(Of course, I didn't hear all that from where I was. Jules just told me it on the way back into the loos. I don't have X-ray ears or anything.)

If I had X-ray ears

111

So then Jules said, "I hope that on Saturday night you can come and stay overnight at my abode (abode is posh for house, BTW) where we can work on our super-brainy project with the help of my mater and pater (mater and pater is posh for mum and dad, BTW)."

So Tilda's dad said he was sure that would be fine and took her number and said he'd give her parents a call to arrange it.

Oh hang on, now Jules is banging on the door. She says she's been ready for ages and what am I doing in here and I've been so long have I suddenly got my Q or something? Sadly, that is not the reason, like I said I'll probably be about 24 when that finally happens. Gotta go,

Byeeeeee!

At home,
later (like, 7.46 p.m.)
(not on loo roll).

I've got to add this bit although I don't want to. I want it to be how it was when the plan was all fabulous and perfect – but when I came out of the loos, Jules dropped a bad surprise on me. Mum calls it a bombshell when people do that, like when Dad told her he was moving out. Jules's bombshell was not a really really big deal like that, but it was still pretty bad. I said, "I'm so glad you like Tilda now," and Jules said:

"But I don't like Tilda. She's a wimp. I'm only doing it for you because you are my BFF and you want to help her."

BOOOOOM!

This is a bombshell because the fact is that I do like Tilda, a lot, and I want her to be friends with both of us. Jules hasn't seen how much fun she was in the changing rooms at *New Look* and when we were getting ready before the disco. Jules has only seen the always-crying and the Charlie-P-taking-away sides of her.

So, it would seem impossible that we could all 3 be friends, but then Jules doesn't know about my brilliant new plan, which is even better than the Makeover Plan and the Strict-Parent-Busting Plan (okay, that one didn't quite work out, but...) and the Julietta the Superswot Reverse Makeover Plan. So, Miss Garcia Perez Benedicionatorio had better watch out, because this is the ultimate plan and it is going to totally make her like Tilda – or else!

For my plan I need some equipment, so I have done a list like in science:

List of Equipment for Top-Secret Friendship Plan

1. Nice notepaper (the strawberry-smelling kind with little purple spirals on).
2. A feather from my silver feather boa.
3. Secret magic chant.
4. Twister board.
5. Sabrina the Teenage Witch and Friends DVDs.

Before I became Mrs. Stepton's favourite, I'd always thought that science was the sort of pointless subject that's no use for solving real problems. But now I have discovered a good reason for it – to help you make people who *don't* like each other *like* each other.

HA-HA-HAAAAAA!

I think you know what that is by now!

1.26 a.m. Saturday night

No, sorry, I mean
Sunday morning.
(How freaky is that?!)

Tilda and Jules fell asleep ages ago, but I just can't stop my head buzzing with all the things that have happened. Maybe if I write it all down it will buzz right down my arm and out my pen and into this journal and then my head will get some peace!

So, yeah, Tilda's dad dropped her off about 7 o'clock. He'd talked to Jules's dad on the phone about the sleepover and because he thinks Jules is in actual fact Julietta the Superswot he was cool beans about it (plus, he didn't know I'd be here, of course!). It was lucky he didn't come in though, because we'd forgotten that he was expecting Julietta the Superswot and not Jules the scruffy-bunchly, purple-stripey tightsy, black-nail-varnishedly Supercool Babe. Tilda wasn't surprised to see me there 'cos Jules had told her about the Sleepover Plan on the phone.

Jules's mum and dad were at that second still out at salsa dancing and so JJ was in charge (YIPPPPPEEEEEEEE!), but we didn't see him at all, because he was being in charge from his room (BOOOOOO!). Actually, he was playing this cool rock music so loud he wouldn't have known if anything emergency was happening to us even if we screamed at, say, 8 million decibels. (How do Benito and Benita ever sleep in this house?!)

In actual fact, I was a bit worried that something emergency *was* going to happen to us when Tilda came in, 'cos she handed Jules her coat like she was the maid or something in olden times. Jules just stood there staring at it, looking like she might drop-kick it into the bin (where there are quite often yukoramic things like cold baked beans and alphabetti spaghetti because of Benito and Benita). Jules was about to open her mouth and create an emergency that JJ wouldn't be able to

hear, but then I looked at her and did my kind of
please-oh-please-be-nice face that I do when the
man in the market has put onions on her hotdog
without asking. So anyway, Jules saw my face and
luckily she just threw the coat on the arm of the
sofa a bit crossly. Then she grabbed a bottle of
Coke out of the fridge and we all went straight up
to her room.

Jules's house is the old Victorian kind, more
than 100 years old in actual fact. Like to us in
England it doesn't seem really old or anything
because we have those houses
from Shakespearean
times that
are made out
of bits of wood
with horse poo
and mud and
straw and that
packed in
between

(we did about it in history but I can't remember what it's called – something that sounds like *wobbly doors*, I think). So, if you live in one of those kind of houses, and if you're reading this in bed, **RIGHT NOW** you could have your head about one and a half centimetres away from some horse poo that's maybe 600 years old! Hmm, luuuuurvley! Bet you're really happy about that!!!

But, you know, Jules's house isn't as old as that, although people from America would think it was ancient because everything's new and drive-in over there. So if you could get a coachload of Americans to come and look round Jules's house you would make loads of *dough* (which is American for *dosh*, **BTW**) and they would all be taking pictures and going *gee whiz* (which is American for *cor blimey*, **BTW**). Of course, you'd have to dress up like in those back-in-time programmes on telly. I can't see me and Jules doing those sewing things that say "home sweet home" or Jules's mum managing without her combi washer-dryer, so we probably won't be getting any Americans round after all.

What was I saying this for? Oh, yeah, 'cos Jules's room is as old as her house (dur, obviously, stupid girl!) and it's got a cool sink in the corner and a little dressing room bit where she keeps all her ripped tights and black webby jumpers and that, but in Victorian times it's where she would have kept her rustly skirts and whalebone corsets and those weird little hats they wore. Those hats wouldn't ever keep your head dry in the rain, so like, what was the point? Maybe it was just 'cos beanies hadn't been invented yet. In actual fact, lots of old people *still* don't know about beanies, 'cos in the rain they wear this clingfilm stuff on their heads tied round under their chins. (Maybe it's also 'cos they are still amazed by The Wonder Of Plastic.)

Sooooo, anyway, seeing as Jules and Tilda hadn't even said 2 actual words to each other, I knew I had to put my Friendship Plan into action *tout de suite* (that's French for PDQ, BTW) (PDQ is English for Pretty Darn Quick, BTW).

So my first plan was to make a nice spiritual atmosphere by chanting about the bounty of Mother Nature. We were supposed to chant to the full moon, but we looked out the window and there was only this tiny slither, so we chanted to Jules's huge Chinese paper lantern instead. We just felt really silly and kept giggling, well me and Tilda did. Tilda said chanting about the bounty of nature was making her want to eat an actual Bounty *bar*. Jules got really moody because she said staring at the light shade was giving her a cricked neck (the other thing about houses as old as Jules's are that the ceilings are so high we had gone all giraffy!) and that it was all stupid anyway.

So my first plan didn't work because Jules got in a dark and stormy mood. She went out into the hall and yelled at JJ to **TURN YOUR *!$**$* MUSIC DOWN!** So JJ turned it up, but then we heard Jules's parents come back in and Jules's mum yelling up the stairs at JJ to **TURN YOUR *!$**$* MUSIC DOWN!** JJ turned it down a bit then, because otherwise Jules's mum would march up there and go all screamy-shouty on him about Benito and Benita and about how he was supposed to be looking after us (not that we need it – we are old enough to be babysitters ourselves!).

So I had to go on to a quick Plan B, which was playing Twister. At first, Jules kept pretending to accidentally fall on Tilda but I know it was on purpose, because she was going "sorry" but she had her good-actress face on. Tilda had her might-be-about-to-start-crying face on, so I was just worrying about how to make the plan work when I had to lean right over them both to get my left foot on blue and I did this big botty burp! Well, we all collapsed in total hysterics and they were both putting their noses in their sleeves and going,

"My God, Lucy, that is disgusting!" And we all just lay there for ages giggling and going *"pwoor"* when suddenly Jules remembered she was in a mood and went, "I'm going to get some Wotsits," really sulkilily (hang on, do I mean sulkingly? Or sulky-like?).

So I said, "Excuse me just one moment, Tilda," 'cos Mum's brought me up to be all polite and then I went to the kitchen to find Jules. Salsa music was coming out of the lounge so I knew that Jules's mum and dad had started practising straight away.

"Jules…" I went, and Jules waved her hand out of the cupboard at me and said, "Do not talk to me, Lucy Jessica Hartley. I am being in a mood."

"It's not a proper mood if the simple fact of someone doing a parp makes you forget to be in it," I said.

Jules went, "Yeah, well, why does *she* have to be here?"

"We are being Stand-up Babes, remember?"

I said. "We are cheering up a girl with" (and then I whispered this bit just in case Tilda had the magic power of hearing past 2 lots of music, down one flight of stairs and through 2 shut doors) *"no friends."*

"Well, as long as we don't have to be her friends," grumbled Jules, and I thought **eeeeekkkkkk!** 'cos that's exactly what I wanted, but I went, "No, we don't," 'cos there's no point making Jules go all screamy-shouty. So I knew I still had work to do, but luckily I had some more plans and when we got back upstairs I brought out Plan C, the feather. No, I was not going to tickle them into liking each other...we were going to try doing some actual magic.

We sat in a circle munching Wotsits and put the feather in the middle. We all stared at it, wanting it to levitate off the ground. We even tried saying spells like in Harry Potter, although that's just out of a book and isn't magic really. Still, we had to test...

Still nothing happened and still nothing

happened, but then Jules went, "Stupid feather," and gave it a poke, and then it was amazing because it did actually start moving! It didn't fly off the floor or anything, but it was sort of trembling and swaying from side to side, *totally on its own*. We all looked at each other and all the not-liking Tilda by Jules was forgotten because we had actually made real magic! But then Jules noticed that the hem of her skirt was moving slightly too and we realized that by poking the feather she'd accidentally moved it into the draught from under the door (that's another thing houses as old as Jules's have – draughts!).

Well, I can tell you that we were so disappointed in the magic not being real. We were probably as disappointed as Mum was about me lying to Tilda's dad or even as disappointed as Tilda's dad was about her going to the disco.

To cheer us up, I said we should make up secret magic names for ourselves and then pass round the pieces of paper so that we could read

each other's, but that we must never say them
out loud or tell them to anyone. I think it's okay
to stick them in this secret journal, though.
Hang on, I'll just reach across my sleeping pals.
Tilda and Jules won't mind me having these
because just a little while after we made them
up a very exciting secret
was told, so they were
quite quickly forgotten.

Anyway after we'd passed them around I
said, "I know we're not allowed to say the name
out loud, but why did you just pick *that*,
Tilda?"

And Jules said, "Not everyone has such a good imagination as me and you, Lu," in her fake-nice actressy voice.

"I *have* got a good imagination," said Tilda. "For example, I can easily imagine you tripping over a pistachio nut and spraining your liver and kidneys, Jules, and maybe having to stay in hospital for a whole year where they only feed you lumpy mash." Jules scowled at Tilda, but Tilda (very bravely) carried on. "It's just, that name *is* magic to me," she explained. "And I'm going to be called it from now on no matter what anyone says. I'm even going to ask Daddy to call me it."

Jules stopped scowling then and just stared at her all gobsmackedly, and I could tell she was thinking Tilda was entering Coolgirlville.

So, the feather levitating was really just the fault of a draught but what Jules and Tilda didn't know was that the *real* magic was working – the friendship magic that I had planned all along. So I laughed the evil-genius laugh (you know, **HA-HA-**

HAAAAAA!) and they stared at me like I had gone loopy, so I quickly said, "Hey, I know, everyone has to tell one secret – their most secret secret!" And that's when the most amazing thing happened.

Oh, wait a sec, I have to go to the loo. Not just to sit on the closed seat either, so I don't think you want me to take this journal with me!

Byeeeeeeeee!

Sorry about that, and at the most exciting bit too!

So, I was saying about everyone having to tell their most secret secret. Jules said she'd go first and I thought she was going to say a real one but she just went, "I'm secretly a vampire and I go out every full moon and hunt for foxes and then I drink their *blooooooooood!*"

I went, "That's not a sensible one, Jules," but she just shrugged and said that was all we were getting.

I was busy glaring at her for spoiling it when Tilda said all quietly, "I'll tell you mine." And then she went out and checked in the hallway that no one was there listening, but the other Garcia Perez Benedicionatorios were either asleep or listening to different music, and Jules's mum kept going "*Yeeeeeeeeee-ow!*" to the salsa.

Tilda shut the door tight and then she said, "Can you put the stereo on just in case?"

Here is a tip – if you don't want other people to hear what you are saying, sit next to a loud noise. So we put on some thrashy rock music and Tilda said something so secret I have written it in code:

".oga skeew eerht doirep ym tog I"

Jules went, "For real? Wow!!"

And I went, "You really got your Q?"

And Tilda went, "Huh? What's a Q?"

And I looked at Jules because I thought she was going to go all huffy on me 'cos it's our secret BFF thing, but she just went, "You can tell her 'cos she told us something really really secret." So I explained about P and changing it to Q so we could talk about it even when boys are there. And we asked her about what it felt like and all that stuff.

Then because the mega-loud music was still

hiding any possible escaping whispers, I decided something. The thing is, Tilda had told a really good most secret secret. So I decided to tell a secret so secret I couldn't even write it down before. I couldn't even, like, think it. But I had to tell, because it's been really bugging me and that's what mates are for, isn't it? So I told them about Dad. Not about his pants and the curry and foot-flavour flat, but I mean about how I was worried that maybe he didn't love me any more. (Wow, I wrote that forwards! Never thought I would do that.)

"Course he does," said Tilda. "It's true that people change all the time, like me turning into Tilda, but *that* won't. You should talk to him about it."

I shrugged. "But I try to tell him things and he never knows what to say."

"That's okay, as long as he listens," said Jules. "I wish my mum and dad would stop talking back and just listen sometimes."

Then Tilda said, "I think my dad would listen, but there's some stuff I just can't tell him."

"Do you mean about Gina Fulcher?" said Jules. Looking at her face I could see she was no longer doing the nice-acting thing, but that she was being really truly a Stand-up Babe.

Tilda bit her lip and nodded, looking like she was going to cry.

"Tilda, it's nothing to be ashamed of," I went. "It's not your fault that Gina Fulcher's a complete idiot with the brain of 2 gnats rubbed together. You should have told your dad what was going on and then he would have known I was a good friend and not a *corrupting influence*."

I felt really sick in my stomach again, just *thinking* of when he said that.

Tilda sighed. "I know I should have. But it's just, well, Daddy really wants me to enjoy school. He'll be so upset if he finds out what's been happening. It's just too hard to tell him."

Jules did an even sweeter thing then. She

hugged Tilda and said, "On your *own* it would be too hard. But not together. We'll tell him tomorrow."

Tilda smiled at Jules and Jules smiled at Tilda and I knew the plan had worked. I would have done the evil-genius laugh but I didn't feel like it. Then we did each other's hair and then we watched the *Sabrina* and *Friends* DVDs and Jules and Tilda fell asleep halfway through Series 3, but I just couldn't. I turned the TV off and stared at the (very high) ceiling for a while, but I still couldn't sleep. It felt weird not having my most secret secret hidden inside me any more and also I was nervous knowing I had to talk to Dad about it.

Then I got kind of hungry so I sneaked out and down to the kitchen. You can usually find some cool stuff called "tappers" lurking in Jules's fridge (that's Spanish for snacks, BTW). They are things like whole prawns and bits of aubergine and Spanish olives and some things that you can't even tell what they are 'cos they're fried in batter so you just have to bite into them and hope there's not too much chilli in there (which, let's be honest, there usually is!).

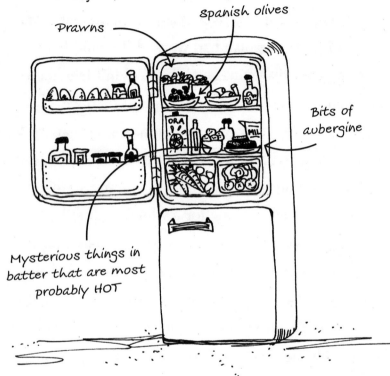

Prawns

Spanish olives

Bits of aubergine

Mysterious things in batter that are most probably HOT

So I was standing staring into the fridge when someone came in. I was about to scream, "Help! Burglar!" when I realized it was JJ. Then I was about to scream, "Help! JJ!" because I realized I had no make-up on, not even the accidental kind, and my hair was all in a scrunchy bundle. So to distract JJ from the total mess I looked like, I went, "Hi, JJ, I have to tell you something. I really fancy you."

Eeeeeekkk!!! How did that come out?! Maybe telling one very secret secret makes others come out all on their own. But it felt nice to say it actually, after all this time of seeing him and just staring gobsmackedly and going "urgle-urgle" instead of proper conversation, or otherwise going on about the danger of manholes for no reason.

JJ did this standing-back-in-surprise thing that was fake but in a sweet, funny way. (Did I mention he's sweet and funny as well as totally gorge??) Then he went, "Lu, you're a great girl, I just—"

And I said, "It's because I haven't got big you-know-whats like Suzanna, isn't it?" (**OMG** I still can't believe I said that!)

And JJ went, "No, but it *is* about Suzanna. She's so much more than just, well, big you-know-whats. She's a nice girl. I really like her."

"So it's just 'cos you like her," I went. "It's not 'cos you don't like me?"

"Course not," said JJ. *You're funny and smart and stylish* (although you should see someone about that obsession with falling down manholes) and in a couple of years—"

OMG I should get that engraved on a plaque!!!!

"What, you think by 2 years' time I'll have big you-know-whats like Suzanna?" I went. (Even now I can't believe I kept mentioning that!!!)

JJ laughed. "No, I was going to say that you'll be old enough to start going out with boys!"

I went all grumbly-huffly then and said, "I am *now*, actually."

JJ squinted at me in the light from the fridge and I was thinking **eeeeeekkkkkk**, don't look too closely! "Who are you going out with?" he asked, all protective-ish. "If anyone messes you around, Lu, they'll have me to answer to."

"No one," I managed to croak.

Then he winked at me and wandered back upstairs. Yes, that's right, he **WINKED** at me – big you-know-whats or no big you-know-whats! And he said he doesn't not like me. That is *soooooo* cool! *Go Lucy! Go Lucy!*

Sunday

It's only 6.41 o'clock but I am
going to bed straight after I
finish this 'cos I'm soooooo tired.

This morning we slept in late then got showered
and dressed and all that, and watched some more
Friends, but nothing that exciting happened until
just before 12 o'clock when Tilda's dad came to
get her. The car pulled up and I was about to hide
out of the way, and Jules was about to transform
back into Julietta the Superswot, but Tilda said,
"No more plans and disguises. You are my friends
now and Daddy can see you just exactly as
you are."

That was so sweet, but still I thought *erk* after
what he said about me being a *corrupting
influence* and I actually didn't *want* him to see
me. So I said fake-casually, "I'm fine with the not
seeing him, actually." Then I said to Jules, "In fact,

have you got anything I could hide behind like a One World display?"

But Tilda got all stricty and said, "No, you're not hiding behind anything."

And I went, "Are you sure? I don't think—"

"Sure I'm sure," said Tilda. "If you hadn't been such a Stand-up Babe, Lucy Jessica Hartley, I would still be a Not-standing-up-for-myself Girl. Come on, let's go." She said it all determinedly and I knew that this was the new kind of Tilda, and she was a bit scary but I liked her.

So we all linked arms and we didn't let go all the way to the front door, even though it was quite hard going down the stairs and through doorways. Well, we let Tilda's dad in and the moment he clapped eyes on me (cool phrase, I'm going to use that more often!) I could see he was like *eeeeeekkkkkk* and the moment I clapped eyes on him, I was even more like *eeeeeeeeeeeeeeeeeeeeeeeeeeeeeeeeeeeeeeeeekkkkkkkkkkkkkkkkkkkkkkkkkkkk* than before. I could tell he just wanted to go,

"What is that *corrupting influence* girl doing here?" But he couldn't because Jules's mum dashed over from the kitchen and kissed him on both cheeks and said nice to meet you and how your daughter is a real pleasure to have to stay and all that.

Benito was running about in his pyjamas driving a remote-control racing car around our feet and Hombrito was barking and there was flamenco music coming from the bathroom where Jules's dad was shaving and some sort of thrashy-metally stuff coming from JJ's room. "You must come in for a coffee, and we should go out dancing sometime and get to know each other," said Jules's mum. "Gabriel and I are learning salsa."

But Tilda's dad just said, "Thank you but we have to go, I'm afraid. Maybe another time."

Jules's mum nodded. "*Bueno*," she said, then she was like, "¡Ay, Benita!" and she went dashing back into the kitchen to stop Jules's little sister from putting frog pencil toppers in the big paella on the stove. Tilda's dad looked around at the mess everywhere and at the real Jules who is not one bit like Julietta the Superswot and then he looked at *me*. His look at me was just *completely* bewildered, like he didn't know what to say at all.

Tilda looked at me and Jules and we did big wide eyes at her, meaning, *say something before he gets all stricty again.*

Tilda took a deep breath and said, "Daddy, I'm not going to stop hanging around with Jules and Lucy. And from now on please can you call me Tilda."

Mr. Van der Zwan's jaw clenched. "Matilda-Jane, we will talk about this in the car," he said firmly.

"I want to talk about it now," said Tilda. "I know I shouldn't have lied to you about the disco. It was a really stupid thing to do, and I'm properly sorry. But I just wanted to have fun like everyone else, and make some friends. It's not fair to judge

141

people on the way they look, or if their families are different from ours."

"We are all One World," I said helpfully, thinking of the display in the front entrance of school, but Mr. Van der Zwan just blinked at me.

Big you-know-whats. Well, if it was a perfect world I would have them!

WE ARE ALL ONE WORLD

He didn't look that convinced actually. I suggested that we all join hands and sing the One World song that 7K did in assembly (which was also when they showed the One World display), but I think Jules's dad's bathroom flamenco must have been up too loud 'cos Jules and Tilda didn't seem to hear me.

"I'm sure you're very nice girls," said Mr. Van der Zwan, in a way like he wasn't sure at all, "but I'm afraid all this lying and deception makes me think that you are not suitable friends for my daughter."

"But they are the *most* suitable friends for me," cried Tilda suddenly. "Only real friends would give me a makeover to help me fit in more, and talk to me in the lunch queue and make jewellery for Gina Fulcher so she stops kicking my bag round the loos and saying nasty comments. And only real friends would dress up as a Superswot to win you over and have me round for a cool sleepover with Wotsits and Coke and

Sabrina the Teenage Witch." Tilda finally stopped talking. Mr. Van der Zwan was staring at her.

"Who's Gina Fulcher?" he asked. "If someone's bullying you, Matilda-Jane, I'll go to the headmaster and—"

Tilda smiled. "It's okay, Daddy. We've sorted it out. It won't happen any more."

"And even if it does, we'll stick together and report it," said Jules.

Mr. Van der Zwan looked like he was going to get even more stricty. But then he took a deep breath and kind of half-smiled at Tilda. "It's a relief to see you so happy," he said. "I've been really worried about you."

Then – how amazing – he half-smiled at *me* too. "I owe you an apology, Lucy," he said. "I thought you were the one making Tilda miserable. I didn't realize you were just being a good friend… in your, ahem, *own way*."

"S'okay," I said, shuffling a bit. How could he

think I was being a bully when I am *soooooo* a Stand-up Babe?! Still, he did say sorry, so maybe he isn't so bad after all.

Mr. Van der Zwan put his arm round Tilda. "How about ice cream in the park, like we used to – unless you have to see your new friends, of course?"

"Naa, Sunday is family day," said Jules. "Loads of people are coming round for a huge meal that lasts all afternoon, and then we're going to evening church."

When she said it, I remembered that there was someone I had to see too. I just needed to give Mum a call and get out of Sunday lunch at Nan's (whoops, I mean Delia's), but I had a feeling she wouldn't mind.

"Come on then, Matilda-Jane," said Mr. Van der Zwan. "Sorry, I mean *Tilda*. You're growing up and I suppose I'd better start getting used to it. Bye, girls."

And so me and Jules both said bye and we

waved to Tilda until the car was all the way down the road. Jules put her head on my shoulder and went, "Can you believe that she told us about her Q – wow, she must really like us!"

So I said, "Yeah, and we really like her too, don't we?" I had to cross my fingers behind my back in hope 'cos knowing how changey-mindy Jules can be, she might have decided not to like Tilda again. But luckily she said, "Yeah. We really do."

Just when I was going, JJ *emerged from his pit* (that's Mum language for *came out of his room*, BTW) and called, "See ya, Lu. Take care. Oh, and don't fall down any manholes, will you?"

"Ha! Ha! Very funny, not!" I went, then I said bye to Jules and shouted thanks to Jules's mum and dad and got Benito's remote-control racing car out from where it was stuck behind the coat stand going *wheeeeeeeeeee* and then I left. As I was walking down the road I realized that when I had looked at JJ leaning over the banister I hadn't gone all wibbly like usual. Maybe I am in actual fact cured of him!!

So I phoned Mum and explained about not being able to come to Delia's (you know, Nan's) for lunch, and she was cool about it. I bet you can guess where I was going instead. If not, the clue is that I had to climb up 4 flights of stairs with all my stuff and then when I opened the door, out wafted the smell of curry and feet. Dad called out from the kitchen, "Hi, Lu. Do you want a drink? I got some lemonade specially, you know, after the beer incident." I dumped my stuff down on the sofa and shouted back, "Dad, I'm 12, not 5." When I got in the kitchen and clapped eyes on him I saw the hurt look on his face. I hadn't meant to sound all stroppy, so I went, "What kind of lemonade?"

He said, "Panda Pops. You always used to like it when you were little. And Alex always loved the cherry flavour."

I couldn't help smiling. He'd remembered

147

exactly what kind of drink I used to like best. My most secret secret about Dad went totally

Suddenly I just knew that he loved me the same as he'd always done. I didn't need to say anything about it after all.

So I got the Panda Pop and we sat down and I told him all about Tilda and Jules and the disco and the Friendship Plan. I wasn't proud of the lying bit, but I wanted him to know the whole story, even the bits that made me look like No Angel. Turns out that Tilda and Jules were right.

Dad didn't have to know what to say — it was just nice that he listened. And I knew he was properly listening too 'cos at one point he even put his guitar down. It was during the bit when I said about Mum leaning on the kitchen surface drinking her coffee when me and Tilda got back from the disco. "So, this Van der Zwan guy," Dad went, all narrow-eyed-ly, "he's married, right?"

I just laughed. "Why do you care?" I said. "It's not like you still love Mum."

Dad shrugged. "Yeah, I know I can't have it both ways. We've got to move on, I suppose. But if any guy's ever not treating her right, you'll tell me, won't you, Lu? 'Cos I'll go round his house and I'll…"

I giggled. "That's roughly what JJ said to me about going out with boys. I thought things might be different when people get as ancient as you!"

Dad laughed. "Nup. Sadly, things are pretty much the same. What else did JJ say?"

"Erm, that I'm too young now but that maybe

149

in a couple of years I'll be old enough to go out with someone."

Dad completely roared. "Clever boy, I like him," he gasped, getting his breath back. Then he stopped laughing and went all serious and looked straight at me. "It's been hard for both of us, hasn't it?"

I had a long stare at my Panda Pop and I thought of what Mum had said about Dad after the disco when she made me that hot chocolate. I said, "Yeah. But that's because you've changed and you want to be someone completely different."

Dad said, "Partly it's that, but partly it's because you're changing too. My little girl's growing up and I'm not handling it very well." He waved at the Panda Pop. "I mean, I know the lemonade is lame."

I took a big swig to prove him wrong. "Really, Dad, the lemonade's great. It's the remembering that counts. You know, things change, but it doesn't mean I love you any less."

Dad looked totally gobsmackedly at me. "Wow!" he went. "That's deep! How did an idiot like me manage to have a daughter as amazing as you?"

I just shrugged but secretly I was totally pleased. "I don't think I'm amazing really," I said. "I'm just trying to say what I honestly feel."

Dad smiled at me and said, "Believe me, Lu, that makes you amazing. And of course, it goes without saying, but maybe I *should* say it for once. I couldn't love you more."

We both got embarrassed then, but luckily Dad quickly went, "Hey, I learned a new song."

He grabbed the guitar and started playing "Are You Gonna Be My Girl?"

Well, if I did have extendable ears (like in that picture I drew before) they would have extended across the room and tried to throw themselves out of the window to avoid hearing the AWFUL RACKET. If Dad wants to be a rock 'n' roll legend he's going to have to spend a lot more time practising strumming his guitar while staring at his pants, plus go to about 87 singing lessons. Sadly, 'cos my ears are not extendable, I had to shout, "Hey, Dad, let's just listen to the CD for now, shall we?"

He poked me in the ribs and went, "Watch it, cheeky!" but he did put it on the stereo and we rocked out all over the flat.

And so I am thinking *yes*. I won't be JJ's girl – well, not just yet. And I won't be the girl of any of the okay boys at school like Jamie Cousins or Ben Jones or Bill Cripps. JJ was right, sort of. Of course, I'm old enough to have a boyfriend if I want. It's just that hanging out with the girls is so much fun I haven't really got the time. Anyway, I'm a busy career woman with loads of brill new outfits to design. So, for now, I'm just going to be Dad's girl.

Anyway, then we flopped back down on the sofa and Dad went, "I know it's not proper Sunday lunch, but how about pizza?"

"Pizza sounds great," I said. "We could split a bit of that garlic bread. You know, the kind we like — with the cheese on?"

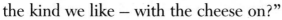

"That's my girl," said Dad.

I smiled a huge big smile and he peered at me, going, "Why the grin?"

"Oh, nothing," I said. "Come on. Let's go."

Is this how you write a yawn?!

Yaaaaaaarugh! ←

Wow, look, I've written *sooooo* much that I've totally run out of pages and only this last little bit of my journal is left. So, I guess this is me, Lucy Jessica Hartley, signing off. I'll buy a new journal and write soon — promise!

Byeeeeee! xxxxx

Lucy Jessica Hartley's BFF Quiz

What kind of friend are you?
♡ Caring ♡? **LOUD**? CREATIVE?
Find out with my fab quiz!!!

1. What do you take for a day on the beach?

A) Cool tankini, shades, lipgloss, suncream, aftersun, fash mags, journal.

B) IPod, black cossie, beachball, frisbee, cheese sandwiches, naughty but loveable dog.

C) Hippy flower-print bikini plus 2 sarongs and giant sunhat (no one is seeing you in just a bikini!!), large Victorian romance novel or advanced maths extension programme workbook 3.

2. Look at the images below. Which one is your favourite?

A)    B)   C)

3. What's your idea of a great evening?

A) A sleepover with your BFF, fash mags and DVDs.

B) A huge family party with friends and dancing.

C) A big bubble bath and a great book.

4. You would rather kiss Simon Driscott than:

A) accidentally get your skirt tucked into your pants at school.

B) get a life-threatening allergy to cheese sandwiches.

C) read something out in assembly (public speaking? Yikes!).

Mostly As: Like Lucy, you are creative and enthusiastic and love to use your talents to help your friends. Just make sure they want to be helped first!

Mostly Bs: Like Jules, you're loud, outgoing and great fun to be with. But give your friends' ears a rest sometimes!

Mostly Cs: Like Tilda, you're a loyal and caring friend, who's always ready to listen. But don't hide in a corner – get out there and enjoy yourself!

Don't miss more of Lucy's hilarious journals

Fantasy Fashion

Lucy's fave mag is running a competition to design a fantasy fashion outfit and Lucy is determined to win the fab prize – whatever it takes!

9780746066904   £4.99

Boy Band Blues

Lucy has been asked to style a boy band for a Battle of the Bands competition and she's mega-excited about it – it's just a shame lead singer Wayne is such a big-head!

9780746066911   £4.99

Star Struck

Lucy's won a part as a film extra and decides she must get her fab design skills noticed on screen – but will the director appreciate her original efforts?

9780746070611   £4.99

Picture Perfect

Lucy decides to throw a big surprise party
for Tilda's 13th birthday – but will crossed
wires wreck her efforts, and their friendship?

9780746070628   £4.99

Style School

School fashion guru Lucy sets up a Style
School in the loos, with lessons in
accessories, hair and make-up. But what will
happen when the School Uniform Police
(aka Mr. Cain) finds out?

9780746070635   £4.99

Summer Stars

The girls are off on holiday and are thrilled
that their fave mag is holding a dance comp
at its beach party in the same town!
Can they strut their stuff on stage and win?

9780746080177   £4.99

catwalk crazy

Lucy is putting on a charity fashion show, but someone seems to be sabotaging all her efforts. Can she track down the culprit and win back her audience before it's too late?

9780746080184   £4.99

COMING SOON...

Planet Fashion

Tilda's bedroom is a design disaster, until Lucy and Jules give it a fab, eco-friendly makeover. But could their green project be gorgeous enough to win them a starring role on Tilda's fave TV show, Go Green?

9780746080191   £4.99

Best Friends Forever

Lucy has decided to makeover the boring school disco into a super-stylish High School Prom. But will she find the right boy to make her big red-carpet entrance with?

9780746080207   £4.99

Totally Secret Info about Kelly McKain

Lives: In a small flat in Chiswick, West London, with a fridge full of chocolate.

Life's ambition: To be a showgirl in Paris 100 years ago. *(Erm, not really possible that one! – Ed.)* Okay, then, to be a writer – so I am actually doing it – yay! And also, to go on a flying trapeze.

Star sign: Capricorn (we're meant to be practical).

Fave colour: Purple.

Fave animal: Monkey.

Ideal pet: A purple monkey.

Best thing about your job: Having to do – ahem – "research" in New Look and Miss Selfridge.

Fave hobbies: Hanging out with my BFF and gorge boyf, watching *Friends*, going to yoga and dance classes, and playing my guitar as badly as Lucy's dad!

Find out more about Kelly at
www.kellymckain.co.uk

For Lucy and Jess

With massivo thanks to my test readers
Tilly New, Hannah and Rachel Munday, Megan
Sambrook-Smith and Ellie Dewar, Hannah and
Rosie Pointer, Georgia Cochrane and Juliet Goss.
You are all Stand-up Babes – mwah!

First published in the UK in 2005 by Usborne Publishing Ltd., Usborne
House, 83-85 Saffron Hill, London EC1N 8RT, England. www.usborne.com

Text copyright © Kelly McKain, 2005.
Illustration copyright © Usborne Publishing Ltd., 2005.

Illustrations by Vici Leyhane.
Photography: Girl, left, page 32 © Heidi Yount/fStop/Getty Images.
Girl, right, page 32 © Peter M. Fisher/CORBIS. Girl, page 33 © Edward
Holub/CORBIS.

The name Usborne and the devices ♉ ⊕ are Trade Marks of Usborne
Publishing Ltd.

A CIP catalogue record for this book is available from the British Library.

JFMAM JASOND/08   ISBN 9780746066898   Printed in Great Britain.